She had been s
moment for a long time...

Nikki had never been this close to Toly's rock-hard physique. They were both tall, and they fit together as if they were made for each other.

Toly smelled wonderful. Nikki loved the feel of his hard jaw against her cheek. It sent darts of awareness through her body. The temptation to turn her head and kiss his compelling mouth was killing her. Toly didn't let her go and she could have stayed in his arms all night.

"If you hadn't been involved with someone else, we could have relaxed like this before an event long before now," he whispered into her hair.

Her heart jumped to think he might have been thinking about her on a more intimate level over the last few months, too. Still, he'd never let her know. They were all friends and she knew Toly kept his cards close to the chest.

But with the way she was feeling right now, he had to know she didn't want to be anywhere else...

and has secretly waiting for

Dear Reader,

Have you heard the famous adage, "Life happens while you're making other plans"?

This is a love story about two rodeo champions who at first seem to have all they could ever want. But of course, they meet with unexpected twists and turns, heartbreaks and disappointments along the way to their happily-ever-after. You'll discover Nikki and Toly having to face shocking events that require true inner strength, and you'll find yourself rooting for them.

Imagine them training for years and years to perfect their skills. Imagine their success coming down to ten grueling nights in the arena in Las Vegas, racing against the clock for the quickest time. Imagine the physical and emotional investments that have been made to get them to that point. Everything has to work. Everything has to be perfect. Right?

Wrong!

That's what you'll discover as soon as you start reading. Enjoy!

Rebecca Winters

ROPING HER CHRISTMAS COWBOY

REBECCA WINTERS

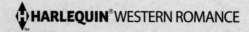
HARLEQUIN® WESTERN ROMANCE

Recycling programs for this product may not exist in your area.

ISBN-13: 978-0-373-75787-9

Roping Her Christmas Cowboy

Copyright © 2017 by Rebecca Winters

Printed in U.S.A.

www.Harlequin.com

Rebecca Winters, whose family of four children has now swelled to include five beautiful grandchildren, lives in Salt Lake City, Utah, in the land of the Rocky Mountains. Living near canyons and high alpine meadows full of wildflowers, she never runs out of places to explore. They, plus her favorite vacation spots in Europe, often end up as backgrounds for her romance novels, because writing is her passion, along with her family and church.

Rebecca loves to hear from readers. If you wish to email her, please visit her website, cleanromances.com.

Books by Rebecca Winters

Harlequin Western Romance

Sapphire Mountain Cowboys

A Valentine for the Cowboy
Made for the Rancher
Cowboy Doctor

Lone Star Lawmen

The Texas Ranger's Bride
The Texas Ranger's Nanny
The Texas Ranger's Family
Her Texas Ranger Hero

Hitting Rocks Cowboys

In a Cowboy's Arms
A Cowboy's Heart
The New Cowboy
A Montana Cowboy

Visit the Author Profile page at Harlequin.com for more titles.

To the continual existence of the rodeo,
a tradition of the American West that's part of
our DNA. May it grow and flourish through the
centuries to thrill young and old alike, as we watch
exceptionally gifted men and women working with
their magnificent horses in a symphony
of unparalleled harmony.

Chapter One

"Come in my office and sit down, Mr. Clayton."

"Thanks, Dr. Moore." Toly Clayton had driven the half hour to Missoula from the Clayton Cattle Ranch outside Stevensville, Montana, for an appointment with a neurosurgeon. He'd just undergone an electromyograph to get to the bottom of the numbness that had attacked his lower right forearm and hand.

"The needle I inserted in your arm muscle recorded electrical activity when it was at rest and when it was contracted. The procedure helped me determine that you have a nerve, not a muscle disorder. How long did you say you've been team roping?"

"I've done that and tie-down roping since my early teens."

"That would explain the numbness that has come on. The constant strain over the years from roping has caused the nerves to be partially compressed or stretched. You say it has happened twice in practice?"

"Yes. Once in October, and again a few days ago. It was frightening to experience that loss of feeling. It only lasted a few minutes, but it was enough to prevent me from throwing the rope with any accuracy."

"Did you feel sharp pains or discomfort in your forearm just before the onset?"

"No. That's what worries me. Both times when it happened, I had no warning."

"You told me in the examining room that you've had no sign of this affecting your feet or legs."

"None. Does that mean I can expect that to happen too? What's wrong with me?"

"You have a very mild form of peripheral Charcot-Marie-Tooth, a slow growing motor sensory neuropathy. It's inherited through a gene carried down in the family. Do you know if you've ever had it in yours?"

"Not that I'm aware of."

"Some people don't even know they have it."

"If it should happen while I'm throwing the rope during a performance at the National Finals Rodeo in December, everything's over for that round and, of course, my partner suffers. We don't get second chances."

"I understand, but if such an incident occurs, you'll still have strength in your upper arm."

"I'm afraid that won't be enough. Is there a medicine to stop this from happening?"

"Not that has been invented yet."

"You mean there's no cure for it?"

"No, but medical science is always working on a cure. I've been doing some research and can tell you they're making strides with a new surgical technique."

Adrenaline filled Toly's system. "You mean there is one?"

"It's been in the experimental stage for quite a while. The results aren't a hundred percent yet."

"What kind of results are you talking about?"

"In a few cases, surgery has slowed down the process. In a few others, it has stopped it."

"What's entailed?"

"The surgery would replace the damaged nerves in your forearm and hand with a new protein that would stimulate nerve cell growth. If successful, it could revolutionize the problem for those afflicted."

"So there is some hope."

"Of course. I'm still doing research on it. The procedure is being done in Paris, France, by a team of neuro and vascular surgeons."

Paris… "If it were possible for me, how long would I have to stay there?"

"Two to three weeks depending on complications."

"When the rodeo is over, I'd like to be a candidate."

"I'm afraid it couldn't be that soon."

"But you will call me when you know anything, and make the arrangements for me?"

"I'll get back to you after I've looked into it more. Just remember it's possible that you'll never have more than the occasional manifestation in your right arm. Call me if you have any more questions, and good luck!"

"Thank you, Dr. Moore. Once the rodeo is over I'll be a full-time rancher and need to get better. You have no comprehension of what it would mean to me to fix this problem."

"If not cured, at least slowed down. We'll talk again soon."

Toly left the doctor's office determined that surgery would help him. Right now he could only hope that he and his partner, Mills, survived the punishing ten days ahead of them.

Anything could go wrong during a rodeo, but the thought of his hand not working for a few minutes had him the most worried. The condition had only manifested itself twice so far. He had to hope against hope it wouldn't come on during their performance.

To Toly's relief, Mills hadn't realized what had happened in practice and he didn't want him to know. Toly didn't plan to tell anyone, not even his family. All he had to do was get through Finals and pray another incident during an actual round didn't cause them to bomb.

Too bad this hadn't happened six months ago. Perhaps he could have gone in for the experimental surgery and be recovered long before Finals. But there was no chance of that now. After the rodeo he would tell everyone he was going off on a month's vacation to do some sightseeing for a change.

If the operation wasn't successful, no one would be the wiser. Life would go on the same. He'd wait until the doctor found another team of surgeons to help him beat the disease.

"IN CASE YOU'RE a listener just tuning in, this is Jeb Riker from KFBR Sports Radio in Great Falls, Montana. It's Friday, December 2, here in Great Falls, Montana. We've been broadcasting our Christmas show from the Ford dealership here in town since two o'clock this afternoon.

"What a turnout we have had to meet the three rodeo champions from our fair state headed to Las Vegas for this year's Wrangler National Finals Rodeo championship!

"All you dudes out there, come on in and meet the beautiful Nikki Dobson. She was last year's Miss Rodeo Montana, and this year's second-place finalist for the coveted national barrel racing championship. I don't see a ring on her finger yet, guys.

"Guess what? She isn't the only eligible celebrity who hails from the Sweet Clover Ranch here in Great Falls. We've got her twin brother Mills Dobson in house. He and his partner, Toly Clayton, from the Clayton Cattle Ranch in Stevensville, Montana, are the reigning team roping champions on the circuit headed for Las Vegas. Ladies? Get ready for this announcement. Both are still single!

"Guys and gals? Don't miss this opportunity to meet these celebrities up close and personal. The next time you see them, they'll be in Las Vegas where they're scheduled to win national championships and be entered into the ProRodeo Hall of Fame."

Wouldn't it be a miracle if that happened. Knowing what he knew now that he'd been to see the doctor, a miracle was what it would take.

Toly looked around the showroom with its lighted Christmas trees, noticing that Nikki had been swarmed by every male in sight. She stood an exquisite five foot nine in her cowboy boots. With her long curly black hair and crystalline gray eyes, she *was* a sight! Ever since he'd asked Mills to be his team roping partner to compete on this year's circuit and had met her face-to-face, she'd blown away all the other women he'd ever known.

In his teens he'd had lots of girlfriends, but his dream had always been the rodeo, ruling out any serious involvement with them. Over the years he'd met literally hundreds of women on the circuit. This last year there'd been a dozen or so who'd caught his eye and he'd done some line dancing with them before moving on to the next rodeo on the circuit.

But always in the back of his mind, the vision of Nikki Dobson got in the way. However, there were several reasons why he'd never acted on his attraction to her. For one, he knew from Mills that she'd been in a relationship that hadn't worked out and was still dealing with her pain.

For another, she was Mills's sister. Though they'd never talked about it, from the time Toly and Mills had hooked up to be team ropers together, he'd sensed that Mills wouldn't like it if Toly showed a personal interest in Nikki. Much as he wanted to, Toly knew he needed to be careful not to let anything affect his friendship with Mills while they were in a competition to win.

Mills and Nikki had lost their parents in a car accident three years ago. Toly had never met them, but he admired the twins who'd overcome their grief and had gotten on with their dreams to be rodeo champions.

Until he retired from the rodeo at the end of this month, Toly would continue to keep it friendly with Nikki. Knowing Mills's feelings, he'd decided not to explore a closer relationship with her...provided she was even interested. He thought she might be. But that was something he had yet to find out while they were all in Las Vegas.

For the next half hour, he kept signing pictures as more fans continued to pour into the dealership. The ladies offered their phone numbers. Toly just kept smiling while they took pictures of the three of them with their phones. Soon they'd be able to call it a night. He wanted to get to bed early. Starting in the morning, they had a thousand-mile drive ahead of them with the horses.

But he never lost track of Nikki who was still being mobbed by guys snapping pictures of her. He imagined she'd had to ward them off since her teens.

"Let's get out of here," Mills suddenly muttered.

Toly jerked his head around. He'd been concentrating so hard on Nikki, he hadn't realized his friend had walked over to him. Since a month ago when the girl Mills had been dating had broken up with him, he'd grown dark and morose. You couldn't even talk to him.

"We'll have to say goodbye to Jeb Riker first and thank the manager of the dealership."

"Yep."

The two of them walked over to talk to the radio announcer broadcasting from the back of a new truck. Toly thanked Riker for the great promotion and send-off. They were joined by the manager whom they thanked and chatted with for a few minutes.

Out of the corner of his eye he could see that Nikki was still involved with her fans. Since she'd come in a separate vehicle from him and Mills, there was no reason to wait for her.

They pulled on their sheepskin jackets and ate another hot dog before working their way through the throng of supporters to the entrance. Once outside, they walked through the brittle snow left by several storms and climbed into Mills's Dodge Power Wagon truck.

The temperature registered twenty degrees and would probably drop to fourteen overnight. Las Vegas sounded pretty good right now with a temperature hovering near sixty degrees.

Mills gunned the motor and they took off, passing Nikki's Silverado truck parked half a block down the street. The silence lengthened on their way to Dobson's small Sweet Clover Ranch on the outskirts of town.

"Want to talk about it yet?"

"Nope."

Toly pushed his cowboy hat back on his head. "If you change your mind, I'm your man."

"Thanks, but I won't."

Until a month ago Mills had been dating Denise Robbins, a girl from Great Falls, for about four months. When she'd unexpectedly called things off, she'd knocked the heart right out of him. Until their breakup he'd never seen Mills so happy. Her action couldn't have been worse for him. At their last two rodeos, his timing had been a little off. Toly had tried to get him to talk about it with no success.

Somehow Toly had hoped Denise would show up at the Ford dealership this evening to make up with him. Toly could have sworn half the town had turned out. She was a former barrel racer and couldn't have helped but hear about it being advertised. With Finals only a few days away, for her to pick this particular time to part ways couldn't have been more cruel.

En route to the Dobson ranch house, Toly received an email notification on his phone from their agent, Lyle. When he checked it, he saw that Lyle had forwarded him an email from Amanda Fleming. She must have gotten his email address off the website that his agent ran for them.

Toly figured she must have sent it from her office at the hotel in Omaha, Nebraska, where they'd met three weeks ago. He and Mills had stayed there while his rig was getting serviced. She had invited Toly to have a meal with her in the hotel after their event and he thought why not. The next day he and Mills left for their next rodeo.

Her email explained that she would be in the stands during the competition in Las Vegas. She hoped they'd be able to spend at least one of the evenings together.

He frowned. She hadn't been on his mind since he'd left Omaha and knew what that meant. Only one woman had the power to remain in his thoughts and not go away no matter what else was going on. That woman was back at the Ford dealership.

Toly was sorry he'd eaten dinner with her. In a few days he would send her an email via Lyle. At that time he would tell her that every night was uncertain because of the gold buckle ceremony and parties after each rodeo. Perhaps there might be a night he was free, but he wouldn't know until he'd ridden in his event. He would have to see. Hopefully she would read between the lines. Toly had no desire to be rude to her, but knew their relationship couldn't go anyplace.

After Mills drove them up to the ranch house entrance, they both went inside and grabbed a snack in the kitchen while they made final plans for the next day.

Toly kept listening for Nikki to come in, but it wasn't meant to be. Furthering his disappointment, Mills informed him that their crew, Andy and Santos, would be driving her horses in their rig. His sister would fly down on the sixth, negating any hope Toly would be able to talk to her at rest spots along their route to Nevada.

Earlier in the day, Toly had made the 190-mile drive from Stevensville to Great Falls in his rig with the horses and he was tired. After staying at the Dobsons' tonight, they would load all four of their horses in the morning and take off on I-15 for their three-day trip all the way to Las Vegas.

The crew would be staying at a hotel near the Thomas & Mack Center and meet up with them on the sixth at the equestrian RV park. It was the place he reserved every year so he could sleep in his rig rather than at a hotel.

This year Mills would be living in the Dobson rig parked next to Toly's rig. Nikki would be staying at a hotel, but during the day she'd drive out to the RV park to exercise her horses. Toly felt a heightened sense of excitement, knowing that she'd be around for those ten days. He would have a legitimate reason to talk to her, coming and going.

After texting his mom that he'd be heading out in the morning with Mills, he said good-night and clicked off. He wouldn't be seeing his family again until everyone flew down for the final night of competition on the seventeenth to celebrate en masse.

Turning to Mills he said, "I'm going to go on up and hit the hay."

"Before you do, come in the den with me for a minute."

Wondering what this was about, he followed him through the cedar-plank-and-brick ranch house to the room where all the Dobson family pictures, awards and trophies were on display.

"Sit down for a minute."

"Sure."

Toly perched on the end of the couch and waited for his friend to speak. Though Mills had darker gray eyes than his twin, their black hair and basic features were so alike it was positively uncanny. They took after their mother he could see in the photographs, but got their height from their father. Every time Toly looked at him, he saw Nikki.

"I've been an ass for the last month. Sorry."

"Forget it, Mills."

"I wish I could." He started pacing, then stopped. "I thought I knew Denise. Geez—how wrong could I have been! I could have taken it if she just plain didn't like me anymore, but her timing after we'd made plans to celebrate when it was all over… I had big plans," he murmured.

Toly had an idea what they were and was heartsick for his friend. "I know, dude. It surprised the heck out of me. I thought you two were tight."

"Join the club. It makes me wonder something. I keep asking myself, did she shut me down right before Finals because *she* didn't qualify and that's why she dropped out?"

"Whoa. I don't believe that, and neither should you."

"I have a reason for saying what I did. As you know, I met her through Nikki. They'd been contestants at the same time for the Miss Rodeo Montana Pageant the year before and became friends. Five months ago she invited Denise to the ranch while I happened to be home that weekend."

"I remember."

"The chemistry between us was amazing. Though you and I were on the circuit part of the time, she and I talked on the phone for hours when we couldn't be together. I thought she was the one."

"Don't I know it."

Mills planted himself in a chair. "What you don't know is how devastated she was when she didn't place in that pageant. For the first two weeks into our relationship, it seemed like all she wanted to do was talk about her disappointment. Then the subject changed when she told me she'd decided to drop out of barrel racing. I'm afraid I didn't immediately connect the dots."

"So what are you saying?"

He took a deep breath. "I'm not sure, but I'm wondering if it's because she's been comparing herself to Nikki and doesn't want to be around her anymore, which means shutting me out. I guess I never told you Nikki made a clean sweep of all the categories in the pageant, including personality, appearance and horsemanship, and she won the Queen Speech award. The folks would have been so proud."

That didn't surprise Toly, who shook his head. Deep inside he had to admit Nikki would be an almost impossible act to follow.

"Look, Mills—even if your supposition contains a kernel of truth and she has some envy issues, I can't comprehend that she would deny herself the happiness you two have found since meeting each other. It doesn't make sense."

"Maybe it does because deep down Denise is more into herself than I'd realized. I found out from my friend José that he went to the same high school with Denise. She was big into barrel racing back then and ran for Miss Teen Rodeo three years in a row."

"How did she do?"

He looked at him. "She never placed in the top three."

"Neither did the majority of the other contestants."

His friend let out a sound of frustration. "But I don't think she ever got over it."

Toly got to his feet. "If that's really true, and you believe she's too obsessed with past failures to see a bright future with you, then she did you a favor by breaking up with you. Let me give you a piece of advice my big brother once gave me. He fell in love with his high school girlfriend and planned to marry her after college.

"But she met an actor from Hollywood while she was in Europe who swept her off her feet. After she came home, she ended it with Wymon. He thought she'd wanted a ranching life with him. It shocked him to realize he could never have given her what she really wanted. But before he finally got over her, he nursed a broken heart for a long time and grew bitter.

"I'm telling you this because when I first got into tie-down roping on the circuit—before my brother Roce and I started team roping—Wymon sat me down because he was worried about me. He knew how much I liked the ladies and feared I might get dazzled too soon by a woman who could never love me. My brother feared that if I wasn't careful, I'd be like he had been and wallow in pain instead of getting on with life."

Mills stared at him. "What did he say to you?"

"To quote him, 'The last thing you ever want to do is get hung up on one of those rodeo beauty queens. They're in love with their own image and probably have been all their lives. The dude who's hooked and can't see through it is doomed to be an afterthought, if that.'

"Later on, I realized he'd said that while he was in a bad place, but after hearing what you've just told me, maybe there was some truth to his words." Toly didn't know what else to say. His friend needed to try to get over Denise or he was going to be miserable for a long time.

Mills stood up. "In the beginning I would never have thought of her like that. But the more I think about it, there has been a pattern of high expectations and bitter disappointments she can't get over. Your brother might have had a point when he gave you that advice."

"Mills? What's important is that you move on for your own happiness."

"You're right. Thanks for the talk. I'm sure as hell

not going to let her ruin what you and I have worked so hard for. I promise I won't let you down."

Toly patted his shoulder. "You couldn't do that. See you in the morning. Try to get a good sleep."

It was great advice to give Mills, but Toly knew he wouldn't be falling off anytime soon. He went back to the kitchen, hoping Nikki would come home so they could talk. No doubt some guy was detaining her.

Starting tomorrow morning, Toly wouldn't be seeing her for the next three days. He wished they were all driving down to Vegas together, but Mills had never suggested it. From the moment the two of them had starting riding the circuit together, Toly had sensed Nikki was off-limits to him. Naturally he was friendly with her when they were all together here on the ranch, but he kept things professional. That's why they'd all gotten along so well.

But Toly wanted more than that. The only thing saving him was the knowledge that the three of them would be together in Las Vegas for ten whole days and nights. He had plans despite what Mills wanted.

After waiting another twenty minutes while he watched the news on the small TV in the kitchen, he decided Nikki might not be home for hours. Not if that dude at the dealership was holding her up.

She could sleep in tomorrow while he and Mills had to take off early. So much for a talk with her before he went to bed. That would have to wait. *Hell.*

Chapter Two

At three o'clock on Tuesday afternoon, the airport shuttle pulled up to the magnificent new Cyclades Hotel and Casino in Las Vegas, Nevada. Four huge, white rounded windmills with their pointed brown roofs and blades—the famous trademark advertising the Greek islands—formed the facade around the entrance. A sign on the marquee said, Welcome Wrangler National Finals Rodeo Finalists.

December 6 was finally here. Nikki climbed out of the limo following her two-hour flight from Great Falls, Montana, and was instantly met with whistles and a barrage of photographers taking pictures. She ought to be higher than a kite to be here at last, on the verge of possibly winning the national championship. But her spirits couldn't have been darker. Not after the conversation she'd accidentally overheard between her brother and Toly Clayton the other night at the ranch house.

She hadn't been able to put it out of her mind and would have given anything in the world for her loving parents to still be alive so she could talk to them about what Toly had said. She was afraid he'd been referring to her when he'd made certain remarks. But there was no such miracle for her and somehow she had to find the strength to get through this experience on her own.

Being a finalist required she had to be prepared to look the part. That meant wearing specific brands like her white Stetson, Justin cowboy boots, and Wrangler jeans and Western shirt. It also meant putting on a smile when it was the last thing she felt like doing.

A doorman reached for her two suitcases and accompanied her inside the lobby decorated with Christmas trees and thousands of twinkling white lights crisscrossing the ceiling. She'd almost forgotten the holiday season was upon them. He put her luggage next to her and went back out in front.

One of the clerks at the counter approached her. "Welcome to the Cyclades Hotel."

"It's good to be here. My name is Nikki Dobson."

The clerk's smile broadened as she signed her into the computer. "You're one of this year's barrel racing finalists. Congratulations!"

"Thank you."

"We have the Delos Island suite ready for you and a rental car. When you're ready to pick it up, their office is down the north hall next to the double doors leading to the indoor pool and gym.

"If you'll follow the bellhop, he'll show you to your room off the east patio. You'll find literature on the coffee table to answer any questions you might have. Here's your card key."

Nikki thanked her again. The bellhop picked up her suitcases and she followed him past a coffee shop and the crowded casino to a set of glass doors at the other end of the lobby. They led outside where a charming, miniature Greek village greeted her vision.

The whitewashed cubed houses built next to each other, with some being double storied, had been designed in the Cycladic style around several swimming pools lined in Greek tiles.

What a stunning change from the high-rises of many other hotels! She liked the architecture and was glad she didn't have to deal with crowded elevators and happy people. After the blizzard she'd left behind in Montana, she had to admit the high-fifties temperature here in the desert felt balmy by comparison.

As soon as she was shown to her two-bedroom suite with its blue-and-white decor, she paid the man for helping her with her bags. If Mills got tired of sleeping in the rig, he could spend a night here in the other bedroom. But in his depressed state, she had no idea what her brother would want right now.

Once she'd closed the door, she sat down on a chair by the coffee table in the small sitting room to text Mills that she'd arrived at the hotel. She knew he was expecting to hear from her.

Next she phoned Santos and Andy, the crew all three of them were sharing. They'd driven her rig and quarter horses here from the Dobson ranch. She knew from an earlier text that they'd arrived at ten that morning and had pulled into the RV equestrian park in Las Vegas. It had several big arenas, nine barns and all the amenities to work with the horses like steer dummies and practice barrels. It saved having to go over to the Thomas and Mack Center all the time where the National Finals Rodeo was being held starting the day after tomorrow.

"How's it going, Santos?

"Despite a flat tire and a long wait while a herd of migrating elk crossed the highway, we're fine."

"Do I want to know how bad it really was?"

"Nope. You've got enough on your mind."

What would she do without their crew. They were her greatest support. "Is Bombshell settling in?"

"She's good. So is Sassy. But Duchess is missing you."

"I'm not surprised. Now that I've checked in to the Cyclades Hotel, I'll pick up my rental car and drive over so I can exercise her."

"That'll perk her up."

"If all goes well, I won't be riding her during the competition. But I need to keep her happy and in shape, just in case of a problem." Though Duchess was fast, she required more cosseting than the other two.

"You can always expect something will go wrong, Nikki."

"Don't I know it."

She'd learned that when her parents had been killed, and again when she realized she couldn't marry Ted, not to mention the pain inflicted when she'd overheard a certain conversation the other night.

As for her rodeo experiences, she'd been riding horses on her own from the time she was seven. Her childhood dreams were all to do with riding in the rodeo one day. At fourteen she'd competed in the teen rodeos.

At eighteen she'd started college and had begun competing on the state and national circuit.

For the last six years Nikki had gone through everything that could go right *or* wrong personally and professionally during her exhausting schedule. It still wasn't over and anything could happen until this competition came to an end after ten grueling nights. Then she'd retire in order to promote the rodeo in a brand-new way with her brother who was also a rodeo champion along with his famous team roping partner.

When the pro rodeo championship finals were over, Mills planned to retire as well and go into business with her. The two of them had talked about it a lot. Neither of them had been lucky when it came to romantic relationships that were destined to last. His recent breakup with one of her best friends, Denise Robbins, had torn him apart. She was glad that when Finals were over, they had each other to rely on for the future.

"Any sign of Mills yet?"

"Yeah. He and Toly pulled in at noon and parked their rig next to yours."

She guessed he hadn't had time yet to answer her text. Technically it was Toly Clayton's rig. They'd lived out of it while doing the circuit this last year. He was the youngest son on the renowned Clayton Cattle Ranch located at the base of the Sapphire Mountains outside Stevensville.

"I'm glad they got there safely."

"Their horses are stalled right by yours. It's a good thing you guys made reservations last January. The place is full up."

"We knew it would be."

"I've already spread several bags of soft shavings in all three stalls. Andy filled the buckets with water and is measuring their intake. When the vet comes around tomorrow, he'll want to check them."

"There's nothing you haven't thought of. Thanks, Santos. I couldn't do any of this without you guys." She got to her feet. "I'll freshen up here, then be over."

"In that case, I'll saddle Duchess and put a soft bit on her."

"Terrific. See you soon."

Nikki hung up, realizing she'd be running into the drop-dead gorgeous Toly Clayton before long. Knowing how he felt about her, it was the last thing she wanted, but being around him was inevitable.

After a year of seeing him coming and going, both on the circuit and at the ranch, she'd thought they were all good friends. But just the thought of him now cut her to the quick.

The other night, on the way to her bedroom after coming home from the Ford dealership, she'd passed by the den, surprised anyone was still up. Toly's words had drifted through the crack in the door.

The last thing you ever want to do is get hung up on one of those rodeo beauty queen types. They're in love with their own image and probably have been all their lives. The dude who's hooked and can't see through it is doomed to be an afterthought, if that.

Stung by words she would never forget, Nikki had run down the hallway to her bedroom so they wouldn't know she'd been in hearing distance. She'd lost sleep that night wondering what that conversation had all been about. But she'd had enough time since Friday to believe that what Toly had said was probably his general opinion of rodeo queens.

In this business he'd met and dated any number of them over the years. After apparently finding all of them wanting since he was still single, it might explain why he'd never tried to get to know Nikki better.

She'd known pain when she and Ted Bayliss realized their relationship couldn't go anywhere. He was a big advertising executive from Laguna Beach, California, who'd asked her to marry him. But he wanted her to move there where they would lead a different lifestyle with his friends that had nothing to do with horses. As he'd said, she could always go back to her ranch on vacations and ride her horses with Mills.

When she told him about the elaborate plans she and Mills had talked about once they'd both retired from the rodeo, Ted recognized that marriage wouldn't have worked for them no matter how attracted they'd been to each other. He had a business rooted in Southern California he couldn't leave. It would mean Nikki would have to uproot herself, something she couldn't do. At that point they stopped seeing each other.

For a time it was hard to accept that there could be no future for them, but she'd finally gotten over it. That's why it surprised her how much she was still hurting over Toly's comments to her brother. It didn't make sense. She'd never been on a date with him or spent hours of time alone in his company, let alone had a relationship with him like she'd had with Ted.

She would love to get into a discussion with Mills about how he felt over his friend's blanket repudiation of women like Nikki who'd been steeped in the rodeo world all their lives.

But in order to bring up the subject with her brother, she would have to admit that she'd overheard the two men talking. She hadn't meant to eavesdrop. After a few seconds she'd fled the scene, but her good intentions didn't matter because Mills would have seen it as an intrusion on his privacy.

After mulling it all over, Nikki wasn't sorry it had happened. What she'd learned had removed the blinders. Toly might be Montana's favorite rodeo champion and a bona fide heartthrob, but his insensitive remarks had ensured she would never be one of *his* worshippers. She didn't care how many gold buckles he'd garnered, or the fame he'd won before he'd ever asked her brother to team rope with him.

Too bad Toly had been her brother's idol for years. The fact that he'd chosen Mills to be his team roping partner for the current year had been a dream come true for him. Though Nikki had every desire to see them win the national finals championship, she would avoid Toly as much as possible.

Nikki wished the side-by-side reservations for their rigs hadn't been made eleven months ago. She couldn't do anything about that. But fortunately she'd be staying at the hotel and not in her rig where she usually slept. The rest of the time she'd be putting her horses through the paces at the park, keeping her distance.

In ten days' time Toly Clayton would be long gone

and she'd never have to see the Sapphire Cowboy again. According to Mills, that was the nickname Toly had been given by a journalist at the *Billings Gazette* years ago when he'd performed as Montana's champion tie-down roper. She'd seen pictures on the billboards driving in from the airport that featured the Sapphire Cowboy on several of them.

Somehow, some way, she had to put him out of her mind. The fact that she was having such difficulty had to mean that on some subconscious level she'd thought a lot more about him than she would have admitted.

Clearly the negative indictment of rodeo queens had been the last thing she would ever have expected to hear on the eve of her hoping to win the national barrel racing championship. That's what you got for listening to something you shouldn't have. *It's your own fault, Nikki. Learn from it.*

On that note Nikki finished the diet soda she'd grabbed from the minifridge and changed into well-worn jeans and a white, long-sleeved cotton pullover. Once she'd stashed her riding gloves in her tote bag along with a bag of peanuts for herself, she put on her white cowboy hat and left the room to get her rental car.

After she'd picked up the Honda Civic held for her, she left the hotel and headed to the RV equestrian park on Flamingo Road. Las Vegas was packed year-round, but during the pro rodeo finals, the traffic was beastly and it could be a nightmare if you hadn't made reservations for everything months ahead of time.

She found the park and wound her way through to their black-and-gold rig parked near one of the barns.

The long white Clayton rig lined up on one side of it had always been Toly's hotel. When she'd first met him, she'd heard him say he was allergic to hotels.

Nikki pulled behind the Dobson rig and got out. So far she didn't see anyone around. Good! She walked around the side and unlocked the door to the trailer section. Before she visited her horses, she needed to load up on some treats for them. They'd been separated three days and needed her love and attention in order to perform at their peak.

A few minutes later with her pockets stuffed with goodies, she walked the short distance to the barn where her horses had been stalled. She greeted Bombshell and Sassy with treats. Tomorrow her three horses would be moved to the stalls at the Thomas and Mack Center for some practice runs.

"There's my Duchess," she crooned to her red roan quarter horse and received a volley of nickers and nudges that made her chuckle. "I missed you too." She fed her some apple-flavored Pony Pops and untied the lead rope to back her out of her stall.

"That's the kind of welcome that makes me jealous," sounded a deep male voice behind her.

Nikki knew who it was. No surprise here when his horses were stalled in the same barn. After taking a deep breath she mounted Duchess, then reached in her jeans pocket for another Pony Pop and turned toward him.

Toly Clayton stood there at six foot three in his boots wearing his signature black cowboy hat that covered a head of dark blond hair. His light green eyes almost blinded her with their intensity.

Damn and blast if her heart didn't rap out a double beat without her permission despite her pain. "I have an idea that will fix all your problems. Why don't you give Snapper one of these on me?"

She tossed the treat to him. To his credit he caught it neatly. They didn't call Toly the greatest header of all the team ropers on this year's circuit for nothing. He was the one who roped the head of the steer. Mills had won the same distinction for being the greatest heeler. His job was to rope the hindquarters. They were both experts. "See you later, Toly."

Nikki rode away, unable to believe he could act like nothing was wrong after what he'd told Mills about her in private. How could he have looked at her just now like she was someone special?

Where did he get the gall to let her think he wanted to be with her and talk to her when deep down he'd mocked her in a particularly cruel way that had cut deep? Now that they were here, she'd be giving him wide berth!

Toly had seen her enter the barn while he was tending to Snapper and wanted to say hello to her, hoping to talk to her for a minute alone. But after tossing him the treat he put in his pocket, she didn't give him a chance to invite her to eat dinner with him and Mills later in his rig.

Though he knew how anxious she was to exercise her horses after being separated from them for three days, he sensed that something else had prompted her to ride off without a normal exchange of conversation. That wasn't like her usual friendly self. Probably nerves had caught up to her this close to the first night of competition coming up the day after tomorrow.

He couldn't help but admire her expertise as she rode Duchess out of the barn. Nikki used a barrel racing saddle with a taller horn and rounded skirt for more stability and control. She had a natural seat that made her look like she'd been born in the saddle. It caused her to stand out when she rode. The fact that she was incredibly beautiful only amplified that picture.

Toly had copped one of her signed posters at the dealership and had folded it inside his jacket so neither Nikki nor Mills could see what he'd done. The photographer had caught her rounding the third barrel at lightning speed during a circuit performance. He planned to put it up in the tack room of the barn at home where he kept some of his favorite mementos.

As soon as she disappeared, he went back to Snapper's stall. After breaking the treat in half, he gave part to him and the other half to Chaz in the next stall. He'd already put both quarter horses through their paces. The two had speed and instincts that made them invaluable.

Once he'd made sure they were watered and had enough hay in their nets, he left the barn. The crew would check on them later. It was four thirty and the sun had just gone down over the horizon. It would be dark before long. Tomorrow the vet would meet him and Mills at the barn to give their horses a thorough exam.

He looked in the direction of the arena. Nikki would be over there putting her horse through a series of backup and turning drills. He would love to watch her, but didn't obey the impulse. She would be back soon.

Toly headed for his rig, but noticed Mills hadn't returned yet. They'd arranged for a rental car and he'd gone to do errands and pick up some steaks to cook. That gave Toly time to let himself inside for a shower and shave before dinner.

A half hour later he got to work on a salad and baked potatoes. He'd learned a long time ago that cooking helped him to relax. As he was whipping up biscuits, Mills came in with the steaks for their dinner and put them on the counter.

"Thanks."

"Sure." He removed his parka. "I saw Nikki's rental car in back. I didn't know she'd texted me until a minute ago. Did she say she'd come to dinner?"

Nope, but Mills didn't need to know what had happened. Toly was still trying to figure out the reason for her unusual behavior. He took the wrapping off the meat to throw them on the kitchen grill.

"I only saw her in passing and didn't get the chance to ask her to dinner. She was in too big a hurry to exercise Duchess. Why don't you call her and tell her it's ready if she wants to join us."

Mills pulled out his cell phone. "That horse has emotional problems. I'm afraid Nikki has taken them on."

"She's a true horse lover."

"Dad used to say the same thing. Sometimes she takes it too far."

"Why do you say that?" Toly put the pan of biscuits in the oven.

"Because she treats them like they're her children."

Toly had noticed that for a long time. It was one of her traits he most admired. "Maybe that's why she's going to win the national championship this time round. There's nothing wrong with those horses knowing they're loved. She's ranked second in winnings and is depending on them to bring her to number one."

"What I'd give to see that happen! No one deserves it more than she does."

Toly couldn't agree more. Both brother and sister deserved that honor. He'd spent a lot of time on their ranch training with Mills, hoping to see as much of Nikki as possible. When she was there, she worked harder to perfect her circles and figure eights than anyone he'd ever seen. The self-discipline she imposed on herself was the reason she was a champion.

Whatever disappointment she'd suffered in love, she hadn't let it affect her standings or work ethic. Toly would like to know a lot more about her personal feelings, but Mills hadn't shared that information with him. Being Nikki's twin, the two of them were careful to protect the other's privacy.

Though it was commendable, Toly was finding it more and more aggravating because his desire to get closer to her had met with a setback earlier in the barn. Something had gone on that hadn't felt right to him and he was determined to get to the bottom of it.

Mills disappeared to talk to her. Toly was forced to live in suspense until his friend came back to the kitchen. "She'll be right over." He started to set the table.

Surprised at the relief he felt to hear that news, Toly turned the steaks and checked on the biscuits that were almost done.

"Later on she has to attend a WPRA party at the MGM Grand," Mills added, "so she won't be able to stay long."

Toly ground his teeth in frustration because after she left, it meant he wouldn't see her again until tomorrow. Throughout the next ten days she'd be staying at the Cyclades Hotel every night. Damn.

THE WRANGLER PARTY for the finalists Nikki had to attend at the MGM Grand would be one of the big highlights during her stay in Las Vegas. For one particular reason tonight that had everything to do with the man in the rig next door, it would be her pleasure to dress the part of rodeo queen to the hilt. She'd brought an overnight bag with her in the car that contained her outfit.

After exercising her horses, she showered in the rig and put on her new Wrangler cream scoop-neck dress with the elaborate crochet back. It fell to the knees. She paired it with ankle-high Italian leather boots in a sand color.

After Mills told her that he and Toly had invited her to come for dinner, she went overboard on her makeup. A rodeo queen's whole purpose in life was meant to knock a man's eyes out, right? She'd do her best to live up to Toly Clayton's preconceived notions, maybe even surpass them. That would be a novel idea. Nikki brushed her hair, leaving it long and flowing. After fastening her new lacy gold chandelier earrings, she put on her dressy cream felt cowboy hat. She'd bought a new handbag to go with her dress and put her wallet and keys inside. One more look in the mirror. The result made her smile. She was ready to do her worst.

She left her rig and walked around to Toly's. They knew she was coming so she let herself in without knocking. Something smelled good. Since her brother wasn't known for his cooking, she had to assume Toly was the chef. Unless they'd bought takeout.

Nikki found them in the kitchen putting food on the table. "Good evening, gentlemen." She put her bag down on the end of the counter. They both turned their heads toward her.

A tangible silence filled the trailer's interior.

"Well, don't all speak at the same time," she teased. "Wasn't I supposed to come for dinner?"

Mills's eyebrows lifted. His face wore the most comical expression she'd ever seen. "Good grief, Nikki."

"What's wrong?"

"Nothing," he said quietly. "You look…nice." He had a hard time getting that word out, making her want to laugh.

"Thanks. Where do you want me to sit?"

"Right here." Toly galvanized into action and pulled out a chair for her. She felt his eyes taking inventory of her face and figure as she sat down. Maybe she *had* accomplished her objective and dazzled him just enough to make him choke a little on his own words.

Mmm. Steak and potatoes. Biscuits too? "Isn't this exciting? All three of us here in Las Vegas at last?"

Nikki glanced at Toly. "By the way, did my Pony Pop do the trick?" she asked after they'd started to eat.

He passed her the tossed salad. "I had to split it two ways, but they both seemed happy enough."

"Next time give them their own packets and see what happens. I've got a ton of them in my rig. You're welcome to help yourself to as many as you want to sweeten things up."

"I'll remember that. Thanks."

Mills eyed both of them. "What are you two talking about?"

"Duchess was overjoyed to see your sister earlier. She gave me a Pony Pop and told me to feed it to Snapper. Maybe he'd be more excited to see me."

Nikki could tell her brother was bewildered, but she was quite enjoying herself and continued to eat. "This dinner is delicious."

"Thanks," Toly said. The man didn't sound happy and she couldn't have been more thrilled. "Would you like a homemade biscuit?"

So he *had* done all the cooking. "Much as I'm tempted, I don't dare. You cowboys don't know how hard we cowgirls and rodeo queens have to work to watch our figures. After trying for so long year after year to stand out in order to be noticed, I'm afraid I'll always be worrying about how I look. It's kind of what we live for, you know? But this steak and salad were perfect for me and have hit the spot."

Mills had stopped eating. He looked sick.

She smiled at Toly. "My congratulations to the cook

who's a team roper too. Imagine me thinking you only knew how to make coffee when we were at the ranch."

Delighted to have delivered that last salvo, she pushed away from the table and got to her feet. "Now I'm afraid I have to go. Sorry I won't be able to help you clean up, but I'm sure you understand I can't be late for the photographers. This party is important because they're setting up a special photo shoot that could open doors for me. You have no idea how eager I am to explore all my new possibilities. Good night, guys. Thanks again for inviting me."

With her cheeks hot from being so worked up, Nikki reached for her purse and left the trailer. She hurried behind her rig and got in the rental car. On her way to the MGM, Nikki relived the last half hour in her mind and was shocked by the way she'd acted. It was like another person had emerged and taken over.

Obviously Toly's conversation with her brother had gotten under her skin and tonight her anger had spilled over. She was incensed for all the women she'd competed with who loved the rodeo and wanted to enjoy every part and aspect of it.

The men who lived and died for the rodeo were no different. They just didn't line up on stage and get chosen as the best or the worst by a committee. Toly Clayton had been strutting his stuff around the country for a long time. His huge fan base fed his ego and was his judge. Who was he to put labels on the women who loved the rodeo and found fulfillment in their own way?

But on the drive to the MGM Grand, her thoughts always came back to the Toly she'd gotten to know over the last year. That Toly had been so fun to talk to. Between rodeos, they'd come back to the ranch and sat around the table in the kitchen to eat after working out.

He was a fascinating conversationalist. They'd exchanged stories about what had gone on while they'd traveled the circuit. He knew everyone's scores and who to watch. So did she. She'd loved the times when the three of them could be together and share their lives. Nikki had grown to look forward to every meeting with him.

But no longer…

She blinked away the tears threatening and pressed on the gas, anxious to get tonight over with.

Chapter Three

Toly could no longer enjoy his meal while he was trying to put two and two together.

Mills had stopped eating and threw his head back. "What in the hell was all that about? I could swear that wasn't my sister who was eating dinner with us a few minutes ago."

"I hate to say it, but I think I know."

"Then you're a prophet."

"Answer me one question. Is Nikki's bedroom upstairs or on the main floor of the ranch house?"

Mills blinked. "The main floor at the end of the…" He groaned and got to his feet. "That's it! She came home the other night after leaving the dealership and overheard us talking about Denise on the way to her bedroom."

Toly closed his eyes tightly. "If she'd listened to our whole conversation, she wouldn't have been angry."

His friend nodded. "You're right. Hell. She heard just enough to send her off the rails. In my whole life, I've never seen this side of my sister."

"Except that she wasn't mad at you. That whole performance tonight was for *my* benefit." It explained how strangely she'd acted at the barn. Now that he knew the truth, he was horrified by the answer.

"I'm positive she happened to overhear me give you Wymon's advice. Taken out of context, his words would have dealt her a fierce blow and turned her inside out. As you said tonight, you didn't recognize your sister. Neither did I."

He threw down his napkin and jumped up from the table. "I've got to find her at the MGM Grand and explain. Carrying this kind of pain has already caused her serious damage. She needs to know the whole truth so she can give the performances of her life out in the arena." He reached for his own set of car keys.

"I couldn't agree more. She's hurting bad, Toly. You go. I'll clean up here."

Toly grabbed his cowboy hat and lightweight jacket, then flew out of the rig to the car. He was surprised he wasn't pulled over by the police while he made his way through heavy traffic to the hotel at top speed. His mind kept replaying the words she'd overheard. He cringed to realize what he'd said about those rodeo beauty queen types. *They're in love with their own image. The dude who's hooked is doomed to be an afterthought.*

He pulled in to the short-term parking area. The first hour was free. He had no idea how long he would be there and kept the ticket to pay later. Once inside the hotel festively decorated for Christmas, he saw that the WPRA party was meeting in the Vista room on the second level and went upstairs.

Men weren't part of this exclusive crowd of women

who were the best barrel racers in the world. From the doorway Toly took in the dressed-up finalists who mingled and chatted with organizers and sponsors. Nikki blew everyone away. She stood talking to several of the finalists he recognized. He found her so breathtaking, he wondered if he would ever get it back. Earlier tonight when she'd walked in the kitchen, her beauty had almost caused him to pass out.

Toly had no idea how long she would stay at the party, but it didn't matter. He planted himself by the entrance to wait for her. Photographers took pictures, but she ignored them and moved around the room. He got the distinct impression she couldn't wait to leave and had only put in an appearance because it was expected.

That was fine with Toly, who couldn't wait to get her alone so they could have a long talk. Another ten minutes and it turned out his instincts had been right. She was the first woman to move away from the crowd and head out the main doors. When she walked past him without seeing him, he called her name.

She turned her head. "Toly?" Her expression changed to one of pure fear. "What's wrong? Has something happened to Mills?"

He hadn't seen that coming. The twins had a special bond of love and were close, but he'd just witnessed for himself *how* close. She would never have expected to see Toly here. Naturally her shock was genuine and it touched him how much she cared for her brother.

But it also caused something to twist in his gut because of the painful reason for seeking her out. She shouldn't have to deal with anything but the coming events out in the arena.

"Mills is fine, but I'm not. We have to talk."

Her jaw hardened. "Not tonight. I'm tired."

"It has to be tonight, but not here," he insisted. "We can do it in your rig or at your hotel."

He could see the pulse throbbing at the base of her creamy throat. "What will you do if I don't cooperate? Tie me up like one of your Corriente steers and haul me off?"

Her sarcasm came as a surprise. "If I have to. It's up to you if you don't want a scene."

Color swept into her cheeks. She started walking. He followed her all the way out of the hotel to her car in the parking lot where she sustained a barrage of whistles from every male in sight. When she unlocked it and got in, he climbed in the passenger side.

"How did you get here?" she blurted.

"I drove our rental car."

"Tell me where it is and I'll take you to it."

"I'll worry about it later."

She turned on the engine. "You don't trust me not to take off and leave you standing there?"

"Frankly no. Not in your state of mind."

"What state is that?" She wheeled around before finding the exit.

"The one that brought you close to clipping the end of that car when you turned too fast just now."

She pressed on the accelerator. "There's no way I'm letting you in my hotel room."

"That's fine with me. As you know I'm allergic to them and much prefer our rigs."

Even having to weave through heavy traffic, it didn't take her long to reach the RV park. She wound around to her rig and parked behind it. He got out and reached the trailer door before she did.

The interior of the Dobson rig was every bit as luxurious and comfortable as his. Mills had told him their parents had invested in it for their children several years ago. It was a damn shame they were no longer alive.

He took off his hat and removed his jacket, putting both on the love seat next to him. She disappeared to her bedroom and came out a minute later without her hat.

"I've already told you I'm exhausted." She sat down opposite him. "Please say what you have to say so I can get to bed."

He learned forward with his hands on his thighs. "During dinner, it was obvious to me you overheard Mills and me talking in your family's den on Friday night. I'm sorry you only heard part of it, the part that offended you. For that I'm deeply sorry and want to apologize."

She crossed her long, elegant legs. "There's no need. You didn't know I was outside the door and you're entitled to your own opinion. I was about to say good-night to you, but I heard you talking and—"

"And you found out enough to—"

"To know your opinion of my kind is held by most of the male population," she interrupted him.

TOLY SUCKED IN his breath. "You know that's not true and you're wrong, Nikki. What you heard was an opinion voiced by my oldest brother, Wymon, years ago when I started competing in the rodeo. He'd been hurt by the woman he'd thought loved him and hoped to marry. In his pain, he gave me advice so I wouldn't get destroyed.

"That speech you heard was *his* speech, not mine. I was trying to comfort your brother who's been knocked sideways by Denise. To be honest, I was hurt for him that she chose to break up with him this close to Finals. Of course, it's none of my business and I'm sure the timing wasn't planned, but he has suffered and it has affected his performance."

Nikki averted her eyes.

"By the time you left for the MGM Grand, I realized you had to have heard enough of my conversation with Mills to infuriate you. In fact, it shows great character that you didn't tell me to go to hell to my face before leaving the rig."

"I came close," she admitted.

He smiled. "I knew that. It's why I took after you and wouldn't let you get away from me before I was able to explain what you overheard. The last thing I want is to see you thrown off during the competition because of the cruel remarks you attributed to my feelings. You couldn't be more wrong, Nikki. In my opinion, no other woman comes close to you in any way, shape or form."

She laughed sadly. "You don't have to go overboard."

"Actually I do." No matter how friendly the three of them had been over the last year, Nikki didn't have a clue how he really felt about her. "What's vital to me is that you believe me. I won't rest until I know I have your forgiveness."

Her luminous gray gaze lifted to his. "Of course. I'm afraid I'm the one who needs to ask forgiveness. It proves how much damage can be done by only hearing part of a conversation I wasn't privy to. My reaction does me no credit, especially when you were trying to help my brother. Let's be honest. Neither you nor Mills had any idea I'd come home."

That sounded like the Nikki who'd taken up space in his heart.

"When we left the dealership, I'd hoped the three of us would all head back to the ranch together. But you were still being swarmed by your fans and Mills decided not to wait for you."

"I was surprised how many people came by to meet us." She got to her feet. "I'm thirsty. Would you like a cola? I think it's all we've got."

Toly wouldn't have cared what it was. She was speaking to him again. "I'd love one."

Nikki went into the kitchen and brought back two cans from the fridge. "I'm sorry I was so rude during dinner, Toly. It's my loss that I turned down your home-made biscuits."

"They're my one claim to fame."

"I happen to know that's not true. You're the one who cooked dinner, not Mills. He would never have thought to add pieces of tangerines and walnuts to the salad, or add cheese to the potatoes."

So she'd noticed. "Will you let me take you to dinner tomorrow after the vet checks our horses? Spending time on your ranch, I know how much you like pasta. I thought we'd enjoy some Mediterranean food at Todd English's Olives in the Bellagio Hotel. It'll be my way of apologizing to you in style."

Her eyes smiled at him. "I'd be a fool to turn down an offer like that. You're on."

"Good. You've made my night."

On his way to the hotel earlier, he'd felt like the bottom had dropped out of his life. He could hardly credit the change in the situation since clearing up a misunderstanding that could have done a great deal of harm to all of them.

"As soon as we finish our drinks, I'll drive you back to the parking lot to get your car."

He wished she didn't have to go. "Can't you just stay here and we'll drive to your hotel in the morning?"

"No. I've got an early breakfast with some of the marketers I can't miss. I would rather get back to the hotel tonight. Mills should be coming inside any minute so he can go to bed. It'll be easy to drop you off on my way."

"Then I'm ready to leave when you are." He stood up and put his empty can in the wastebasket.

She left hers on the counter and went back to the bedroom for her things. Before long they were on their way.

"We haven't had a chance to talk privately about Denise. Do you have any idea why she broke it off with Mills? I don't mean to pry. If you don't feel comfortable telling me, I understand."

"I wish I knew." That sounded honest. "She hasn't called me since they stopped seeing each other."

"Would you like to hear Mills's theory?"

"Yes!" she cried. "We usually share everything, but not about this. I've been worried sick about him."

"He thinks she's so jealous of you, she can't be around you anymore. Since you and your brother are so close, it forced her to call things off."

"What?"

"I was shocked too."

"That *couldn't* be the reason, Toly!"

"I don't want to think it, either. He has accepted it's over, but it's sad that she did it so close to the competition."

"I thought so too, but decided there had to be another reason she's not telling anyone. You can tell my brother it's not because of me. I don't think it's about him, either. I know she cared for him a lot and is the sweetest, kindest girl in the world."

"That's what he thought."

"He can still think it! Something's not right. We became close friends. One of these days we'll learn the truth. For her to call him and tell him she couldn't see him anymore means something traumatic had to have happened. But I know it's killing Mills. He's never cared for another girl like this."

"He'll feel better knowing you believe in her."

"I do." They'd reached the MGM Grand. "Where are you parked?"

Toly gave her directions. She stopped in front of his car. He turned to her. "Thank you for giving me the chance to talk to you."

"I'm glad you insisted. I have to admit I was hurt.

It's a lesson I've needed to learn so I'll never let anything like this happen again."

"You were pretty scary at dinner. Mills looked green."

"Don't remind me. I'm ashamed of acting like a woman scorned."

Toly burst into laughter. "To be honest, you not only fascinated me, you were dead-on about my lack of talents."

She shook her head, causing her flouncy black hair to swish across her shoulders. "I didn't mean it."

"I believe you, but it's true. I've been so obsessed with the rodeo, when it's all over I'm going to have to work at becoming a participating member of the human race again."

"That makes two of us. We have to be terribly boring to people who've never been around horses and never want to be."

Now was the perfect time to ask her a question Mills hadn't been able to answer. "Your brother told me you were in a relationship a while back that didn't work out. He's been worried about you. I guess that's the nature of being twins."

He heard her soft chuckle. "We do far too much thinking about each other and try to solve each other's problems. It's worse since our parents died. A psychiatrist would tell us it's not healthy, but we don't know any other way."

"My brothers and I aren't so different, even if we aren't twins. Our father's death changed our lives too."

"Tell me what happened."

He'd never shared this with anyone outside of his family, but it felt good talking to her about it. "I'll never forget. My dad had taken me hunting up in the Sapphire Mountains. We'd camped out for a couple of nights and I'd never felt closer to him.

"He'd been a rodeo champion and knew how much I loved the sport. During our talks he encouraged me to go for it if that's what was important to me. I could earn money to pay for my college and enjoy the sport at the same time. I loved him for being so understanding. On our way down the mountain, he suddenly fell over. Blood poured out of his head. I knew immediately he'd been shot."

"Oh no, Toly! How horrible."

"It was the worst thing I ever lived through."

"I know how you felt. We got the call from the police that our parents had been killed in a head-on crash. The pain of knowing they're gone and you're absolutely helpless to do anything about it is unreal."

Toly nodded. "Exactly. I called my brothers and they came with the sheriff. There was nothing to do for Dad. He'd died immediately. One bullet had wiped out his life. The authorities investigated and discovered it had been a freak accident by another hunter. It changed our lives."

"Oh, how I know that. I'm so sorry for your loss, Toly."

"I feel the same about yours."

"You can tell Mills that Ted Bayliss is long gone from my life with no lingering regrets. It wouldn't have worked. But if my brother hears that from you, he'll believe it. I don't know if you've figured it out yet, but you're more or less the final word with him. I'll reveal one more secret in case you weren't aware. The great Toly Clayton was always his idol."

So many revelations at one time had made Toly's night, particularly the knowledge that she was no longer hung up on the man who, according to Mills, she'd come close to marrying.

The way he was feeling right now, he was ready to rope the steers lined up for the next ten nights at unheard-of speeds. Talk about leaping tall buildings in a single bound—

He got out of the car. "Thanks for bringing me back. I'll follow you to your hotel to make sure you get there safely. Looking like you do, you need a bodyguard."

"That's heady talk." She flashed him a smile that sent his pulse skyrocketing before he shut the door and got into his car. During dinner he never expected to see a smile like that from her again.

Toly turned on the engine and followed her all the way to the Cyclades Hotel. He waited while she parked her car in the lot. After finding a space nearby, he got out of his to walk her to the entrance.

"You don't have to do this, Toly."

Yes, he did. She looked like a miracle of femininity. He wanted to be with her as long as possible. "I feel like it."

"Thank you," she said when they reached the doors.

"Good night, Nikki. Don't forget dinner tomorrow. I'll see you after the vet leaves the stalls."

"Sounds good." There was a moment of hesitation

before she turned to walk inside. He wondered if she'd wanted to invite him to her room to talk some more, but had controlled the impulse.

Toly walked back to his car, determined that there were going to be lots of talks over the next ten nights, either in her hotel room or his rig. Tonight they'd achieved détente. This was just the beginning.

NIKKI GOT THROUGH her next busy day in a daze because she knew she'd be seeing Toly for dinner. So much had been going on in her head after she'd gone to bed, she hadn't fallen asleep for a long time. The old adage about love and hate being two sides of the same coin had taken on new meaning.

Last night she'd left for the MGM Grand so upset, she couldn't imagine calming down. While she'd attended the party, she'd realized what a pathetic fool she'd been to let that anger go on any longer. Wasn't it the truth that eavesdroppers never heard good of themselves.

Before she left the room, she'd decided that tomorrow she would concentrate on improving her skills. How else to come in with the shortest time possible around the barrels every night? Nothing else was important.

Then she'd seen Toly outside the Vista room entrance and her anger had spiraled, almost sending her into shock. Yet once they'd ended up in her rig and he'd explained the situation that had turned her inside out in the first place, everything changed. By the time he'd walked her to the front entrance of her hotel, she hadn't wanted him to go. Faster than she could believe, Toly had become the most important man in her universe.

After the vet had checked out all their horses, Toly had told her he'd be by her hotel at six and meet her in the foyer. From there they'd drive over to the Bellagio.

Though she willed her heart to behave, it still thudded out of control when she saw him walk through the hotel doors at six. He wore a tan Western suit with a cream shirt and a gold-and-silver bolo tie with gold cords.

Toly's handsome features and hard-muscled physique made him striking in a way that prevented Nikki from noticing anyone else. His light green eyes roved over her features. It was crazy how her breathing quickened.

"You're right on time." She could smell the soap he'd used in the shower.

"I've been waiting for tonight and you look sensational. Let's go."

He cupped her elbow and walked her outside to his car. Nikki was glad she'd bought the black skirt and black short Western jacket with the colored red embroidery and fringed sleeves. It had been worth the steep price to evoke a compliment from him.

Toly had booked their table in advance at Todd English's Olives. Once they reached the Bellagio, they weren't kept waiting long. Throughout their dinner of succulent beef carpaccio and ricotta ravioli, he hardly kept his eyes off of her. She had a difficult time not staring at him too.

"Do you know what Mills is doing this evening? He didn't answer my text."

"He met up with friends after doing some shopping."

It wasn't like her brother not to answer. The poor guy wasn't acting himself, but she knew Denise was the reason why. "I did my shopping in Great Falls."

"I think he left it until now so he can walk off his nerves."

"I'm sure you're right. Everyone has their own way of coping before competition."

"Well, I don't know about you, but being out to dinner with the most beautiful woman in the restaurant has made me forget everything else."

She smiled. "Flattering as that is, I don't buy it. For the last hour I've noticed you flexing your right hand off and on during our meal. If I didn't know better, I'd think you were imagining yourself on your horse, waiting for the gate to open while you figured out how best to rope your steer."

His eyes narrowed. "Only a pro like yourself would catch me out."

"I've watched my brother long enough to know he goes through roping scenarios in his head, even when he's talking to me. He gets this vacant look."

Toly laughed. "I know it well. Are you ready to order dessert?"

"Not tonight. I need a good sleep and the extra sugar will keep me awake."

"I'm passing on it too. Shall we go?" He signaled the waiter for the bill, and they left. "Tomorrow's our big day," Toly murmured as they made their way back to her hotel.

"Don't I know it. I want to thank you for getting me through tonight. The dinner was delicious."

"The pleasure has been mine." He parked the car and took her arm to walk her inside. His touch sent a current of electricity through her body. Their eyes met one more time. "I'll be cooking dinner again at four thirty tomorrow. Why don't you join me and Mills before we head on over to the Mack Center? Before you say no, just keep in mind it's a great relaxer for me."

"When I have the time, it is for me too. Thank you, Toly. I'll come if I can leave my last scheduled party soon enough. Good night."

She turned and headed toward the other end of the foyer. Though she didn't look around, she could feel his gaze on her. It gave her the kind of delicious shakes she'd heard about all her life, but had never experienced until now.

Nikki was in love with him and knew it. That's why it had almost destroyed her to hear what he'd told Mills in private. Yet somehow she had to handle her emotions while she was facing the most challenging moments in her career as a professional barrel racer.

Being in love with her brother's roping partner had heightened the stakes. When she reached her hotel room, she found she was breathless reliving the events of the evening with him. *Toly, Toly.*

Chapter Four

After Toly returned to the RV park, he grabbed some horse treats out of his rig and walked over to the barn where he found Mills inspecting his favorite horse. His friend barely acknowledged him. Toly stood near the stall. "What's wrong with Atlas? The vet already checked out our horses today."

Mills lifted his head. "He's fine. Where were you tonight?"

He frowned. "I took Nikki to dinner as my way of apologizing to her. Didn't you get my text?"

"Nope."

"That's strange." Toly pulled out his phone and checked it. "Damn! I wrote it, but didn't press Send. Here. Take a look."

"Forget it. I believe you."

"Did you and the guys go to dinner?"

He nodded.

Toly gave his own horses a pat down before he walked over to Mills who was settling his other horse Dusty for the night. "Want to tell me what's going on with you?"

Mills looked at him hard. "My sister wouldn't have gone to dinner with you if she weren't interested."

His head jerked back. Where had that come from? "She agreed to go because she knew I felt terrible about what happened. It was my way of making it up to her."

"No." He walked out of the stall. "She went because she wanted to."

He felt as if he'd been gut-punched. "I thought you were glad I drove to the MGM Grand to talk to her."

"I was, and I'm thankful she was able to forgive you because that's the kind of person she is. Maybe too forgiving."

Whoa. "Mills? What's going on with you? Since when was it wrong for me to ask her to dinner? Talk to me!"

"I'm not saying it was wrong. But because it's *you*—the cowboy who can have any girl he wants at any time and walk away until the next one comes along—I'm worried. My sister isn't that kind."

A prickling of anger started at the back of Toly's neck. "You mean she's not like the groupies. Don't you think I know that? I've never gone out of my way to attract her attention."

"I know. That's the hell of it. You're a magnet. That Amanda Fleming you met during the last rodeo? Lyle sent me some emails and said she's in Vegas and has emailed you more than once on our website. All you had to do was have one dinner with her, and she's back for more. But you and I both know you never plan to see her again."

Toly couldn't believe what he was hearing and it

hurt like hell. "I had no idea you've resented me for such a long time."

He shook his head. "I don't resent you, Toly. Not at all. But I can see what's happening to my sister and I'm scared you're going to hurt her more than she's ever been hurt in her life."

"You honestly think I would do anything to cause her grief?"

"Not intentionally. The guy she fell in love with hurt her so badly, she's really fragile."

That wasn't the impression Nikki had given him. But he could see Mills was a mess right now. "Shall I uninvite her for dinner tomorrow afternoon before we all leave for the rodeo?"

Mills's eyes darkened. "You asked her?"

"Wasn't that the plan while we were here in Las Vegas? Eat our meals together before each event? Isn't that what we decided before we drove here? What's changed?"

Mills looked stone-faced. "Has she already accepted?"

"She said she'd come if she could get away in time from another party she'll be attending."

He looked down. "You can be sure she'll do whatever she has to do to be there, so it's already too late to tell her not to come."

Toly had to think fast. "We can send a message right now that dinner is off because you and I have been talking and need to go over to the center early tomorrow."

"No. You can't do that."

"Then what do you want me to do, Mills?"

"I wish the hell I knew."

"That's not a good enough answer. Talk to me."

Mills squinted at him. "I guess it's because Dad isn't around. He'd give her the kind of advice she needs. When I try to talk to her, she doesn't take me seriously."

"What advice is that?"

His jaw hardened. "That she needs to concentrate on her rodeo career before she gets involved with another man." He turned abruptly and strode out of the barn.

Ninety-nine percent of this reaction had to do with Denise's rejection. But the remaining 1 percent convinced him that Mills didn't want Toly to be that man. Was that because Mills didn't like him personally and didn't think he was good enough for Nikki? That thought hurt.

The two of them needed to work this out before too much more time passed. After saying good-night to his horses and giving them some treats they devoured in record time, he followed after Mills.

But when he knocked on the rig door, his friend didn't answer. At that point Toly walked to his own rig and phoned Wymon. To his relief his brother answered and they talked about everything.

"Sorry that my advice to you years ago has caused problems now."

"Ironic, isn't it, when it was such good advice for me back then?"

"Bro—I've known you've been in love with her this last year. Not in so many words, but I've recognized the signs. And Mom has moaned at the way you've spent so much time at their ranch to train."

Wymon understood a lot. He wasn't the older brother for nothing. "Yep."

"I'm sure Mills has sensed it."

"I realize that, but I don't know what to do. What a time for this to happen with the competition starting tomorrow!"

"Tonight he exploded with nerves and everything else. But *he's* got to be the one who figures that out, Toly. Not you. He knows you didn't do anything wrong. By morning he'll have cooled off and probably apologize. He's a good man."

"I *know* he is."

"If you want my advice, until you leave Las Vegas, be your friendly self to him and Nikki. Do what you always do and concentrate on winning that championship. Don't change anything. If Nikki can tell he's trying to come between the two of you, let *her* be the one who goes to her brother. No one will ever be able to reassure him the way she can."

Toly took a deep breath. "Thanks, Wymon. I needed to hear that."

"One more thing. I'm glad you've finally admitted you're in love. Be assured I won't tell anyone else. Good luck tomorrow night. We'll be watching you on TV. I'm counting on all three of you coming in first!"

DURING THE EARLY hours Thursday morning, Nikki's crew transported her horses to the Mack Center stalls. She worked with them before all the finalists met to rehearse for the arena parade that would take place that evening. Toly and Mills had the honor of carrying the

Montana flags for their event. Laurie Rippon had won the right to hoist the Texas flag for the barrel racers.

With the rehearsal over, she left for the Cowboy Gifts Party, but didn't stay long. After going back to the hotel to shower and pack a bag, she drove to the RV park to join Mills and Toly for an early dinner in his rig. Once again she could smell food cooking when she walked inside. Toly was at the stove.

"Hi!"

His head turned. "Hi, yourself!"

"I noticed the car missing. Where's Mills?"

"His glove got a rip in it today during practice. He ran out to buy a new pair. I expect him back pretty soon."

She walked through and sat down at the kitchen table. He'd already made blueberry muffins and urged her to try one. After a first bite she ate the whole thing. "These are wonderful. I'm addicted already."

"Good. I've got a roast cooking with potatoes. It'll be done before long."

"There's no hurry. I haven't stopped all day. It feels good to sit."

"How was the Christmas party?"

"Wonderful, but crowded even if it was staged at the South Halls Center, or maybe because it was." She chuckled and eyed him covertly. "Have you had a chance to tell my brother about my thoughts where Denise is concerned?"

Toly poured them coffee and sat down. "Yes. He's reserving judgment, but I know it made him feel better to hear that you felt there was another explanation for why she broke up with him."

"I don't think anything could improve his spirits right now."

He studied her for a moment. "How about yours? Tonight we'll be posting our first scores. Are you ready to knock them dead?"

"Don't I wish, but I'm not worried about you and Mills. You've averaged number one going into Finals. I'm positive you're going to win the whole thing."

"*I'm* not." The fear that his hand might lose feeling at the wrong moment was haunting him more and more. "Did you check out Shay Carlson's last couple of scores? He got a 3.90 in Oklahoma. We're going to have to do better to win."

She moaned. "I hear what you're saying. I've got to beat Laurie Rippon. At the Austin rodeo I got a 13.57 on Bombshell. That was my best score this year, but Laurie turned in a 13.49 and is in the number one spot going into Finals. She's the one who makes me the most nervous."

"You can bet she's scared of you being in second place. So little separates the two of you."

"I know." She sighed.

"This is the hard part, isn't it? Anticipating the odds. Waiting for it to start."

"It's awful." She needed to stay busy. "I'll set the table." Nikki finished another muffin. "I really put my foot in it when I refused your biscuits the other night. You knew I was a fraud."

His eyes lit up in amusement, sending curling

warmth through her. "But while you were making your point, no one could have topped your delivery. Did you say you were the number one debater in your high school?"

"Are you kidding?" She burst into laughter.

"You could have fooled me."

She knew when he was joshing her. Nikki tried to remember the last time she'd had this much fun, but she couldn't.

He darted her glance. "Tell you what. Since your brother hasn't come yet, let's go in the living room to wait for him. I'm in the mood for cards. What's your game?"

This was going to be fun. "Anything."

"Is that right?" He sent her a wicked smile.

"Yep."

"I get to pick the penalties."

"I think we should take turns on that."

She felt his chuckle resonate inside her.

"How about a little music?" He turned on the radio to some soft rock and reached for a deck of cards before they sat down at the little table.

"I wonder how many cards games have been played on this?"

"Thousands," he said with a poker face.

Nikki shook her head. "That wouldn't surprise me."

He grinned. "How about pontoon?"

"Great! It's kind of like blackjack. I love it."

"Shall we say a set of twenty rounds to start? If I win, you'll have to dance with me. If you win, you'll have to dance with me."

That set Nikki off laughing and they played a fast, slap-down hysterical game. To her surprise she did win, but that didn't seem to bother Toly who pulled her out of the chair into his arms without giving her a chance to think about it. "Um. This is nice."

Nikki felt his words in every atom of her body. She'd never been this close to Toly's rock-hard physique and had been waiting secretly for this moment for a long time. It was a far cry from line dancing where there were separations in their togetherness. They were both tall and they fit together as if they were made for each other.

He smelled wonderful. Nikki loved the feel of his hard jaw against her cheek. It sent darts of awareness through her body. The temptation to turn her head and kiss his compelling mouth was killing her. Toly didn't let her go and she could have stayed in his arms all night.

"If you hadn't been involved with someone else, we could have relaxed like this before an event long before now," he whispered into her hair.

Her heart jumped to think he might have been thinking about her on a more intimate level over the last few months too. Still, he'd never let her know. They'd all been friends and she knew Toly kept his cards close to the chest. But the way she was feeling right now, he had to know she didn't want to be anywhere else.

They both heard a car door slam at the same time. "That'll be Mills," she murmured in silent protest. His arrival had saved her from making a fool of herself in a grand way.

She eased herself away from Toly and hurried back to the kitchen. He followed her. The time spent with him for the last hour had been a bit of heaven she hadn't wanted to end. Last night her anger had flowed like lava. Tonight she was mush in Toly's arms.

If her brother had seen them dancing together with no air separating them, it would have shocked him and she wouldn't have blamed him for that reaction.

Mills opened the door and came in the kitchen. "Hey, guys."

Nikki eyed her brother. "There you are! I heard you had to buy a new pair of gloves."

"Yep. One of them got ripped. I found a new flex knit kind that are thinner and easier to work with. Not so much bulk." He stood at the sink to wash his hands.

"Do you wear that kind too?" she asked Toly.

He sent her a slow smile, as if he too was remembering what was going on before Mills came in. "No. Since I'm the header, I have to have the heavier Kevlar glove for protection."

"I didn't realize. You learn something new every day." She turned to Mills. "We're glad you're back."

"Come and sit down, dude. Our dinner's in the oven waiting for you and we're starving."

"I got held up with a couple of friends."

"That's okay. You were gone longer than we thought, so we started a card game. Your sister beat me."

Toly took out the roast and put it on the table. Nikki could see he'd arranged potatoes and carrots around it and they'd cooked in the juice. Her own mother couldn't have done it better. "That looks scrumptious."

"I need a lot of protein along with carbs."

She'd witnessed that at dinner last night when she'd wished they could have spent all night together. "Don't we all, and plenty of snacks throughout the day."

It was fun to eat and talk shop with the top team roper cowboy on this year's circuit. With the kind of regimen they had to keep, there was nothing to explain. They could read each other's minds.

Besides not being completely in love with him, this was yet another reason she could never have married Ted. It would have meant giving up the world of horses. Being with Toly like this let her know more than ever that being with a man like him was the life she wanted.

Toly slanted her a glance. "I was hoping the three of us could play another set of cards before we have to leave for the center."

"I'd like that too." She struggled to keep the throb out of her voice.

"It's too late," Mills muttered.

Well...that solved that.

Nikki's brother was being impossible. Trying to lighten the mood she said, "Tomorrow I'll cook dinner just to make it fair. You guys will eat in our rig. I can plan our meal a little earlier so we can play a game of pontoon before we leave for the arena."

Toly nodded. "I hope you meant that, because now that you've offered, I'm not going to let you out of it." His tone excited her. She saw a glint in Toly's eyes, thrilling her more than anything because it meant the feelings she was experiencing weren't only on her part.

"Mills?" she prodded him. "Does that sound good to you?"

"Sure."

Sure? He wasn't only depressed, he was downright rude. "I like to cook," she continued, "and it will give Toly a break. Maybe my brother will even volunteer to help me?" she said to get a reaction, but none was forthcoming. They settled down to eat and she passed Mills some blueberry muffins.

"Don't mind if I do." He took one and devoured it, but he was unusually quiet.

Nikki smiled at Toly. "You really are a great cook."

"At least I'm good for something."

Upset at Mills by now she said, "You two looked great out there today carrying our flag. I've never been more proud." Her heart had swelled with pride to watch the two of them race into the arena like the champions they were. Tonight there'd be fireworks and ear-deafening cheers from the packed center.

"You didn't look so bad yourself," her brother finally murmured.

"Well thank you for the overwhelming compliment. On that note, I'm going to go in the bedroom and get ready before we drive over to the arena."

If any of them won a gold buckle tonight, they'd pick them up at the South Point Hotel. Every night after the Wrangler National Finals, the public could watch the Go-Round Buckle Presentations. She had no doubts Toly and Mills would come in the top winners, but a first-place win for her was iffy.

"Hurry—" her brother interjected. "Otherwise we'll be late for the parade. I'll drive us over."

She had it on the tip of her tongue to remind him *he* was the reason they needed to rush now. But she held back and noticed that Toly had already started to clean things up.

"Give me a minute to put on my gear and I'll meet you outside." Nikki had a special Western shirt to wear with fringe and the ProRodeo insignia. After running a brush through her hair and applying lipstick, she was ready.

On the way out of the trailer, she reached for her white cowboy hat and put it on. Toly held the door open for her. "If you don't know it yet, you take my breath away," he whispered.

Much as she wanted to believe it, she was afraid to, not after her brother had told her Toly was *the* ladies' man on the circuit and always had been. How many other women had he said that to over the years?

She hurried out to the car where Toly was already standing. In a low voice he said, "With your long legs, you should sit in front." On that note he opened the front passenger door for her. No woman could be immune to the smile he flashed at her. "I'll sprawl across the backseat. Shall we go?"

Nikki climbed in and fastened her seat belt while she contemplated his flirtatious comments that took her mind off the coming event. Toly had a way of completely disarming her.

They were off to the Mack Center where the crowds were just about impossible to get through. Mills had radar eyes and found an empty space behind the center where all the trailers were parked.

This is it, Nikki Dobson. It's what they'd all killed themselves for and dreamed of. She got out of the car and they made their way into the rear of the building.

When they reached the inside, the three of them had to part company. She lifted her eyes to them. "Good luck, you guys."

"The same to you," they called after her.

Her heart was in her throat as she hurried off to mount her horse and line up in the alley prior to the parade.

Tonight Nikki had decided to ride Sassy, her palomino. In her tan Western shirt, they matched. As her father had once said, this horse had shown sass from the beginning, prompting Nikki to give her that name. She was a showstopper and handled crowds and noise like a trooper. Not only that, she was fast and would explode down the alley into the arena.

Andy and Santos met her at the stalls. They had her horse saddled and bridled with her softest bit to prevent pain from the rein tension. She walked up to Sassy and pressed her face near her ear. "Tonight's the night we've been working for, my girl," she crooned. Her horse nickered. "I know you're going to give me your all."

She fed her a Pony Pop from her pocket and Sassy chomped away, causing the three of them to chuckle. It was time. She pulled her gloves from her pocket and mounted her horse. Sassy had been through this routine earlier in the day and knew what was coming.

Making a clicking sound, she led her horse through

the aisle to the back of the center where everyone was lining up according to their event. Nikki passed several of her competitors. They all smiled and looked fabulous. She swallowed hard to think she'd reached this milestone.

She looked for Toly, but couldn't see him because his group would be entering the arena long before hers. The music had started and the announcer was welcoming everyone to the Wrangler National Finals Rodeo. Between the noise and the fireworks, in her opinion, there was no buildup or excitement like it anywhere in sports.

Nikki patted Sassy's neck and kept talking to her while they waited in place for their turn to come. She spotted Laurie up in front carrying the Texas flag. It was almost their turn. "Remember what we're here for," she whispered to Sassy. "There's no horse like you. Act like someone and show your stuff!"

Suddenly her group started to move and they took off down the alley. The thrill of it sent a rush through Nikki's body. As they poured into the arena, the announcer named each contestant.

"Here comes Nikki Dobson in second place from the Sweet Clover Ranch in Great Falls, Montana. She's the former Miss Rodeo Montana riding her palomino Sassy."

The crowd went crazy and Nikki had to admit this was one experience she was thankful she hadn't missed while living on this earth. She raced around to her spot and drew up next to Laurie. At her other side was Portia Landwell, the number three finalist from Nebraska. Before long, all hundred-plus finalists were on display.

She doubted any of the pageants during the Middle Ages with their knights and pennants were any more spectacular and colorful than the sight of these superb athletic national champions carrying their flags and decked out in all their Western finery. Nikki felt great pride to even be a part of this, no matter if she came in last at the end of the ten days.

As they left the arena the way they came in, she caught sight of Toly carrying the Montana flag and leading their group with Mills who also carried a flag. Toly was a magnificent sight wearing a black Western shirt and his black cowboy hat. As far as Nikki was concerned, the quintessential male rodeo performer from the Clayton Cattle Ranch left everyone else in the dust.

Tears smarted her eyes before it was her turn to leave and exit the arena with the speed of the wind. Sassy was in her glory. Nikki had endowed her horse with human feelings. Maybe it was silly, but she didn't care.

When she reached the stalls, the first person she saw was Toly. He was still mounted on Snapper, but minus his flag. Their eyes met for a quiet moment. She knew he was seeing the look of elation on her face that illuminated his own countenance. Joy radiated through her being that they were experiencing this once-in-a-lifetime moment together.

His event would take place before hers, but it wouldn't be long now. "Go get 'em, cowboy."

"I intend to," he answered in his deep, rich voice. "But I'll be back to watch you cut circles around those barrels with the precision of a surgeon." Then he was off to win what she felt sure was their first victory for tonight.

"Nikki?" Santos called to her. "Are you all right?"

She turned to look down at him. How could she possibly answer that question when her heart was so full of emotions? The only thing she could say was yes.

Taking a deep breath, she led her horse down the aisle and walked her around until it was time for her event. There were screens in the back so she could watch the other events. She said a special prayer when she saw Toly and Mills were up next. But she had to wait because the first-place winners had to compete last.

She couldn't move as she watched and listened as they flew out of their gates with the steer running between them. Toly threw a butterfly loop with lightning speed and Mills was right there to finish up. The crowd went wild when it was announced they took first. No surprise there. Toly did it in 3.7 seconds and Mills in 3.8.

Beyond thrilled for them, Nikki mounted her horse and got in line. Soon her event was announced. "You've got to fly like the wind, Sassy girl. Here we go!"

She made a clicking sound and they were off with her heart thudding. They shot down the alley and out into the arena. Her mind was on Toly's words to cut those precision circles. But as she went around the first barrel, she felt something was wrong and corrected too late, losing time.

As she rode home, she saw her score and knew it wasn't good enough to be first. In a few minutes she learned Portia had brought in the top score, with Nikki a disappointing second. This score kept her at her second-place average. Her thoughts flew to Sassy who'd lost time. It meant Nikki had done something wrong, not her horse. Nikki realized she'd been in too big a hurry.

The guys came to congratulate her. She kept a smile on her face as she congratulated them. "I couldn't outdo you."

"You will," Toly assured her. "This was only the first night."

Mills hugged her and told her the same thing.

Together they drove to the South Point Hotel. Nikki loved watching them receive their gold buckles to the ear-splitting applause of the audience. She told them that if they wanted to party, she'd take a taxi back to the RV park. Both of them declined, saying they were tired and the three of them drove back to their rigs.

Nikki jumped out of the car ahead of them, needing quiet time to understand how to fix what had gone wrong tonight so it wouldn't happen again. "I'm so proud of you two, but now I have to get back to my hotel. I need to get up early and exercise the horses before tomorrow night's event.

"Don't forget, you guys. My turn to fix dinner. Come at four!" She hugged her brother.

Toly followed her to her car. "We'll be there. If you want to talk now, I'll come to your hotel."

There was nothing Nikki wanted more than to be alone with him, but Mills was waiting for him in their car.

"Thank you, Toly, but I'd prefer to get back and just crash."

"That's a good plan too. I've done it many times. Blot

tonight out of your mind and start again tomorrow. But if you want to talk to me earlier tomorrow, you know where to find me."

She nodded.

In an unexpected move, he kissed her cheek and walked away before she got in her car. The touch of his lips on her skin sent tingles of delight through her body. She was still feeling the effects after she got in bed an hour later. Nikki finally fell asleep, longing for the moment when she felt his mouth on hers.

Chapter Five

Toly knew Nikki had suffered a huge setback tonight.
Second place would never satisfy her, but she'd put on
such a great front while they'd been out celebrating,
you would never have known it.

He couldn't fully enjoy his first-place win with Mills,
knowing how disappointed she had to be. As for Mills,
he'd been in a bad place for a long time. Now with his
sister's second-place win, he would be worrying over
her even more.

"I'm going to bed, Toly." No small talk from Mills
tonight. That was just as well. Toly wasn't in the mood
for it, either.

"I hear you. See you in the morning." He watched
Mills walk to the Dobson rig until he disappeared.

Toly felt like he was in an impossible situation wanting to be a good friend to Mills without revealing what
was in his heart about Nikki.

After reaching for his gold buckle, he locked the
car with his set of keys and entered his own rig. As he
walked back to his bedroom, he read the half a dozen
texts from family and close friends who'd sent their con-

gratulations. Hail to the conquering hero. His brother Roce's well-meant message rang hollow. At one time Roce had been his partner until he gave up the rodeo to start veterinarian school.

Never had Toly felt less jubilant, not when his soul was so torn and conflicted. His interest in Nikki was part of the reason Mills couldn't pull himself out of the blackness. But there was no way Toly could stop caring about her any more than he could stop the sun from rising in the morning.

He'd told her he'd wanted to drive to her hotel and talk to her face-to-face. He ached to comfort her. After being with her earlier and dancing with her, he realized that he needed her in his life on a constant basis. But she'd said she'd wanted to go home and crash.

Had she told him that because her brother would be aware of it? Since they couldn't be together tonight, his only choice was to do the next best thing. After showering, he got in bed and phoned the Cyclades Hotel. Toly had never asked for her cell phone number, so he had to go through the operator and hoped Nikki picked up. At least he could say good-night to her one more time.

"I'm sorry, sir, but Ms. Dobson isn't answering. Do you want to leave a message?"

He debated for a moment. Maybe she wasn't in her room yet. Maybe she *was,* and fighting off deep pain. But when he thought about it, the things he wanted to talk to her about needed to be said in person.

"No. Thank you."

Any conversation with her would have to take place tomorrow. In the morning he'd give Mills some space and go to the local gym he always frequented. He'd work out to strengthen his lower right arm until he felt like dropping. Afterward he'd run his horses through some light exercise while he waited for four o'clock to roll around.

Knowing he wouldn't be falling asleep anytime soon, he turned on the TV and watched an old *Indiana Jones* movie until he knew nothing more.

FUNNY HOW NIKKI had been living to perform at Finals, yet as soon as she'd finished her late Friday morning workout with the horses at the center, she'd rushed to the store to buy groceries for their dinner. This was her night to cook for Toly and wanted it to be special. Knowing she'd be seeing him shortly helped put last night's second-place finish behind her. She knew what she had to do to come in first.

Meat loaf and scalloped potatoes were big hits with her brother at home. She was sure Toly would like everything. But she didn't have time to make yeast rolls, so she bought the kind that all you had to do was let the dough rise and then bake them.

While she was putting the potatoes together, she heard a knock on the trailer door. Nikki left what she was doing to answer it.

"Toly—" He stood there with a twenty-inch-tall Christmas tree covered in tiny ornaments and lights.

"Merry Christmas!"

She couldn't believe it. "What a surprise! You're early! We won't be eating for another hour."

"I know, but Mills is still outside putting Atlas

through some more training exercises. My horses have done enough for one day. After practicing some loops on the dummy steer set up in the RV park, I didn't have anything else to do and thought I'd come and bother you. Maybe play some more cards with you."

She smiled. "The champion team roper who won last night didn't have one thing to do?"

"Nope. I had such a great time at our dinner last night, I want it to continue." *So do I, Toly. So do I.* "That is if you'll let me in."

"Oh—sorry. Of course." She was so thrilled to see him, she wasn't thinking clearly. "Forgive me. Come in the kitchen with your Christmas cheer. You can put it on the end of the counter and plug it in."

He set it up easily and the lights went on. It touched her heart that he'd been so thoughtful. "I love it! Thank you!"

"You're very welcome."

"Want some coffee and a doughnut?" She'd picked up half a dozen of those too.

"Thank you, ma'am. It's just what this cowboy needs."

She hurried to pour him a cup and told him to sit down at the kitchen table. After placing a plate of doughnuts in front of him, she put the potatoes and meat loaf in the oven. Once she'd fixed coffee for herself she joined him and munched on a doughnut. As usual they devoured carbs to stay energized.

In his Western shirt and jeans, Toly was so hunky she couldn't believe he'd come over just to hang out with her. It was like a dream come true to have him all to herself before Mills showed up. The tree made it seem like this was their little home, filling her with happiness.

Nikki studied him for a minute. "I'm sure you're going to win the championship this year. What I want to know is, did Mills speak the truth when he told me you're really going to retire from the rodeo when this is over, no matter what?"

When he said yes, it was after a long silence.

That seemed odd to her. "Would you mind telling me why?"

He sat back in the chair, eyeing her over the rim of his coffee mug. "I'm needed on the ranch full-time."

She considered his answer. "Not that it isn't a good reason, but is it your only one for walking away from the sport that has put you on the map? You've got more great years ahead of you. I'm curious."

A thoughtful look crossed over Toly's arresting male features, as if he were considering what he wanted to tell her. She wondered what had caused his hesitation in the first place.

"You've been in this business a long time like me, Nikki. We both know where the rodeo is headed. Team roping is the most popular event among amateur participants. The fans relate to the sport better than anything else in rodeo.

"Yet off the top of my head I can think of four Professional Rodeo Cowboys Association rodeos around the country that offer a shootout-style performance outside of the PRCA that *exclude* team roping, and in most cases tie-down roping."

She nodded. "I'm very much aware of it. I've seen

the same problem with barrel racing. It isn't always included unless the Women's Pro Rodeo Association is involved. You know, the traditionalist's view of rodeo. I find it interesting that team roping was only added as a Professional Rodeo Cowboy Association standard event in 2006. Though a casual fan might not notice the exclusion of an event, an active one will know the difference if it's not included."

"Exactly, Nikki. You take those elements away and you're weakening it. Shoot-out rodeos that eliminate those venues are becoming the new sensation, bringing in a bigger market, especially on television." He poured more coffee for them. "One of my rodeo friends, Buck Slidell, said the attendance at the Houston Livestock Show and Rodeo in March was down 16 percent from fourteen years ago."

"I heard it was because of cost-of-living expenses across the state, but that can't be the only reason."

"It's part of it, including higher gas and utilities prices," he stated. "In the end it means some families won't spend any extra money on the rodeo. The same problem has hit many states, and money isn't the only problem. Bad weather keeps people away. There are so many other activities like Friday night football and baseball, fans have to make a choice of where to go and it isn't always the rodeo."

Nikki stirred in her chair. "Not to mention complaints that the live entertainment at a lot of rodeos doesn't feature enough big singers and bands. Even bull riding, which is a fan favorite, can't fill the stands without the right musical acts. And I heard some of the guys complain in Austin that the rough stock events were fouled up by a mix of dairy calves with Angus. It was a mess. The list of problems goes on and on."

"But it's the team ropers and tie-down ropers I'm the most concerned about if they become a casualty in the shake-up. It's safe to say that no one in the industry understands or is aware of everything that is happening on every level. I know I'm not. For me, seeing the sport contested at the highest levels with the ropers and barrel racers is part of what keeps our dreams alive."

"For me too," she concurred.

"But the PRCA is trying to gain a new audience and push rodeo to a new level of television coverage. It's been tough the last few years with all the big rodeos wanting to limit some of the venues." He swallowed his second cup of coffee. "I hate to see that happen. Progress has a way of changing the dynamic in all the areas of the sport."

"I know."

"I've had the time of my life since I got into it. But I've decided it's time to get out before the fragmenting because of money and world market interests dilutes the whole scope of things."

She nodded, even though she felt there was still another reason he didn't care to divulge. "I've been thinking a lot about that since the talk I had with my brother. Ages ago we decided that after retirement we'd go into business together to run our own rodeo and perpetuate the events we love.

"Even three years ago I was sure a venture like that would be successful. But because the world is changing all the time, it's impossible to see into the future. Which means it's going to take more effort to keep it alive."

He reached across the table and grasped her hand. Her breath caught from the contact. "There will always be the rodeo, even with animal rights activists making their protests. We just have to be prepared to make accommodations and move with it."

Nikki heaved a sigh. "Except that I'm afraid I'm a purist and want things to be like they were in the past. I know I sound like my grandparents. They hate cell phones and want life to go back to a slower pace. I've never been able to convince them that new advances in technology have transformed the world. They just look back at me with sad eyes because I don't understand."

Toly smiled before letting go of her hand. "Before my grandparents died, they expressed the same thing. I remember them telling me they felt sorry for me because I hadn't grown up in their world. It was the golden age to them, even with the Depression."

She laughed gently. "Now I find myself feeling the same way about what's happening with rodeo trends."

"But the rodeo will never go away, and we'll have our memories of this year's Finals to treasure."

Nikki was beginning to get teary-eyed because she'd never known this kind of happiness before. She'd always admired Toly from a distance. But because he shared her passion for the sport, she loved being able to talk to him intimately like this. To think this time would never come again brought her pain.

"You're right, Toly. And now I'd better get this show on the road if we expect to eat." She got up from the table to take their meal out of the oven and bake the rolls when she heard the door open. "That'll be Mills."

"I'll make sure."

She heard the two of them talking for a few minutes before her brother came into the kitchen. He looked around. "You've decorated for Christmas!"

"Toly brought it to us."

Instead of commenting, her brother flicked his gaze to her. "What can I do to help?"

"Set the table maybe?"

"Sure." He grabbed the remaining doughnut and demolished it before getting busy. "Something smells good. How come you've been cooking up a storm?"

"Because I like to cook. Toly needed a break. Maybe *you* will even volunteer one night. Hot dogs and chili?" But the minute the words came out, both she and Toly laughed knowing that would never happen.

Her brother didn't join in. "How long have you been here, Toly?"

Did she detect an edge? She guessed that his first-place win last night hadn't compensated for a broken heart.

"Long enough to bother your sister." For the last year they'd all enjoyed a good-natured camaraderie. It was so sad that Mills's unhappiness continued to stand out, making her uncomfortable.

"That's not true," she blurted. "He brought Christmas into the trailer. While we've been waiting for you, we've had a fascinating discussion about the future of the rodeo with its ups and downs. As Toly said, we just have to be prepared to move with it."

Mills put the cutlery and plates around. "Let's not spoil this year's competition by getting on that subject."

Oh dear. Her brother really was in pain and it wasn't about to go away. Thankfully Toly's phone rang, interrupting the conversation. When he picked up, he put it on speaker.

"You've called at the perfect time, Mom. I'm in the rig with Mills and Nikki. She's taking fantastic care of us. Tonight she made meat loaf and scalloped potatoes. We're just sitting down to eat before tonight's event."

His family took turns talking. Each brother sounded excited for them. His mother spoke at the end. "Congratulations on last night's scores. Good luck to all three of you tonight! We'll be watching you on TV. God bless."

Toly's little niece Libby shouted good luck, making them all laugh before they hung up.

Nikki smiled at Toly. "She sounds so cute! Do you have a picture of her?"

"I've got a bunch on my cell."

"While we eat I want to look at them."

Her dinner was a great success. She passed around the rolls. While everyone ate their fill, she looked through his photo gallery. "Oh, Toly, she's adorable."

"She's Eli's daughter from his first marriage."

"Is that her dog?"

"No. Daisy belongs to my brother Roce. He's the vet."

"I could use him here to find out what's wrong with Sassy." She scrolled to the next photo. "Oh—the dog only has three legs."

"It's a sad story. Daisy got caught in a bear trap, but

she functions like any normal dog and is so devoted to my brother it's pathetic."

"How sweet. Ah…and there's another darling baby."

Toly nodded. "That's David, Eli and Brianna's son. They're so happy it's sickening." Nikki chuckled. "He was named after our father who died a few years ago."

It wasn't fair to lose parents so early in life. She kept on going through his photo collection, more and more aware of Mills's silence. "You have a lovely mother, and all you brothers bear a strong resemblance to each other. Their wives are beautiful."

"I agree."

She gave him back his phone and started to do the dishes. The guys helped and before long they were ready to leave for the Mack Center. After changing into her denim blue Western outfit for tonight, she unplugged the Christmas tree lights and hurried outside with her hat.

This time Toly said he would drive. She scrambled into the backseat, forcing her brother to get in front where he would have more leg room. On their way into town, Mills looked at her over his shoulder.

"I saw you working with Bombshell today."

"Yes. I'm riding her tonight. Usually Sassy is so stable. Maybe something's wrong with her, but after thinking it over, I've decided I came in too fast around that first barrel and didn't rate her properly. Not getting her into the right position lost me some time, so I practiced that technique with Bombshell. After I talked to Andy about it, I figured I'd give Sassy a rest and see if I can't get a win with Bombshell tonight."

When Mills didn't respond, Toly said, "I think you're smart to trade off. You've still got nine more nights to bring in the lowest scores. I'm going to switch horses too and ride Chaz tonight."

Nikki leaned forward and patted her brother's shoulder. "What about you?"

"I'm sticking with Atlas."

"He's a great horse." But her comment didn't prompt Mills to do any more talking.

They reached the center and walked inside. Toly smiled at her. "Here we go again. You don't need luck, but I'll wish it for you anyway."

"The same to the two of you." She looked at her brother before kissing his cheek. "Love you."

"Ditto."

Oh, Mills... When they headed for the stalls, she took a different turn and walked out to the stands. The team roping event would be coming up soon. Nikki didn't want to miss it. For a little while she could pretend to be a spectator and melt into the crowd.

Her tension grew while she waited for the guys' event to start. Since they held first place in the standings, they wouldn't come out of the alley until last.

One by one the fifteen finalists took off. Up came Shay Carlson and his partner who were second in the standings. He was the roper Toly wanted to beat.

Nikki held her breath as they roped their steer. Shay did it in 3.8 seconds, his partner in 4.0. Those were the same scores they'd made last night. She'd been keeping tabs. Now it was Toly's turn.

The second their names were announced, the crowd

went crazy. So did she. Crazy with excitement and love for him. The gates opened and Toly flew out on Chaz. Over the years she'd learned that the header set up the run. If he didn't get the steer turned, it was all over. Mills called Toly the quarterback of their team.

Her brother was right. She saw Toly line up the steer so perfectly, a 3.7 score flashed on the counter. *Yes!* To her relief Mills wrapped it up in 3.8. They won the night. Again!

Ecstatic at this point, she hurried back to get ready for her event. She entered Sassy's stall to show her some love and was rewarded with a nicker. "You have tonight off. Enjoy the rest."

She patted her, visited Duchess and walked around to Bombshell's stall where Andy was checking the saddle. He had her horse ready to ride and turned to her. "I have a feeling this is going to be your night."

"I hope so. Thanks for everything, Andy."

After mounting her horse, Nikki patted her neck. "How's my girl? You know what's going on and don't fool me. We had a good workout today and you're going to help me win tonight, right?"

Andy laughed when Bombshell nodded her head, as if she understood her words. Maybe she did, but the nodding was the endearing way this horse always greeted Nikki. The different personalities of her horses delighted her.

"Let's go for a walk and get ourselves ready." Andy patted the horse's rump as they moved out of the stall toward the alley. She could hear the roars from the crowd. The tie-down roping was just finishing up. Nikki got in line in front of Laurie to wait. Her heart was still pumping hard from her adrenaline rush after seeing Toly's score.

Suddenly the line was moving. Another few seconds and her name was announced. "Here's Nikki Dobson from Montana in second place, riding Bombshell tonight!" A roar went up from the crowd.

"Here we go, sweetie. Come on. Let's do it!"

Chapter Six

After the team roping event, Toly had worked his way through the crowd to the front row where he could watch the barrel racing. Mills followed him, still uncharacteristically silent. With another first place and another gold buckle, he'd hoped his friend would be more animated, but such wasn't the case.

They heard Nikki's name over the loudspeaker. Like a shot, she found her first target and circled the barrel so fast, her beautiful hair flew like a black banner beneath her white cowboy hat.

He couldn't believe his eyes as she rounded two more barrels on Bombshell. The only way to describe her action was poetry in motion, an old cliché that couldn't be improved upon. She sped toward the alley in a record time of 3.43 seconds. *Incredible!*

Her rival Laurie rode last, but she took a little bit too much time around the first barrel and came in at 3.67. He let out a whoop of joy and turned to Mills. "She did it! Nikki won! Come on. Let's go back to the stalls to congratulate her."

Mills had become a man of few words, but when

they saw Nikki, who'd just dismounted, he hurried toward her and gave her a long hug. Toly saw tears on her cheeks and hung back. This was a huge moment for brother and sister.

Andy and Santos were there to take care of her horses and gear. Pretty soon a couple of her competitors crowded around to congratulate her. Suddenly Nikki's gaze met Toly's. Her heart was in her eyes. For a moment it was as if everyone else had disappeared while they communed their joy in silence.

He took a step closer to her. "Are you ready to head for the victory celebration? It's your night."

"Yours, too," she said. "I watched you out in front and doubt anyone can beat you two now."

It meant everything to know she'd been there when she could have watched on one of the screens. Naturally he wanted to win the overall championship, but he wanted that same prize for her too. It had become of vital importance to him. He felt euphoric. "Come on. Let's go collect our gold buckles."

Mills said nothing as the three of them made their way out of the center to the car. Nikki climbed in the backseat. "Toby Keith is performing tonight, guys. I hope he sings 'I Wanna Talk about Me.' It's my favorite. Hilarious!"

On the way to the South Point, Toly sang the lines of the song with her pretty much off-key. How funny that he knew all the words too! It was such a unique song and both of them were laughing by the time they reached the hotel and went inside. The crowd went crazy over all the rodeo winners, and then came the entertainment.

Toby sang the song Nikki loved as part of his set. Throughout the number Toly kept looking at Nikki, who smiled back several times. It was a night he would treasure forever and knew the reason why. He was desperately in love with Nikki Dobson, the woman who was here while they shared this magical night together.

Before they decided to leave, Toly checked the text messages his family had sent him. On the way back to the RV park, he conveyed their congratulations to Mills and Nikki.

He was aware his friends didn't have their parents to revel in the excitement. But the lack of animation on Mills's face told him his partner was thinking about Denise. There wasn't a damn thing Toly could do about that, much as he wanted to.

Once he'd parked the car he looked at Nikki, knowing she would be leaving for the hotel. The three of them got out with their buckles and walked her to her car. With Mills there, Toly couldn't tell her all the things on his mind.

"Drive safely," he said. "Dinner in my rig tomorrow."

"I'll be on time."

Those words helped him keep his sanity until he could be alone. After she drove away, he turned to Mills. "We did good work tonight."

"Yep."

Just yep?

"See you in the morning." Without trying to talk to him further, Toly entered his rig. He would wait until

Nikki got back to her hotel, and then he'd call her. But once inside, his phone rang. It was Lyle.

"Toly? You've received several thousand emails I've been trying to keep up with, including three more from Amanda Fleming. She's staying at the Excalibur Hotel and hopes you'll call her there."

He let out a sound of frustration because he'd forgotten about her. "Message received. I'll take care of it." They chatted for a moment before he hung up and called her hotel. To his dismay she answered the phone when the operator put his call through.

"At last!" she exclaimed. "I've been dying to talk to you. I was beginning to wonder if you ever saw my emails."

"Hi, Amanda. I'm flattered that you would keep trying to get through to me."

"I came all this way to watch you perform. Is there a night we can get together?"

He had to make a quick decision. "Tell you what. I don't have any nights open, but if it's convenient, I'll come over to your hotel in the morning and meet you in the coffee shop. It'll have to be early because my day is full. Shall we say eight thirty?"

"You're really that busy?" The disappointment in her voice was palpable.

"Afraid so. Tomorrow morning is the only free time I'll have while I'm in Las Vegas." He ought to tell her the truth now, but after taking her out for dinner a month ago following his rodeo event, he felt he had to explain in person.

"Okay, I'll look for you in the morning."

"Good. I'll see you then." He rang off and phoned Mills who answered on the third ring.

"What's up?"

Toly explained about Amanda and Lyle's phone call. "Do you want to drive me into town in the morning? I plan to tell her I'm not interested, and won't be longer than a half hour. Then we can head over to the center. Or I can come back for you."

Quiet reigned. "What time?"

"I told her I'd meet her in the coffee shop at eight thirty."

"I'll drive you."

"Thanks. See you in the morning."

Toly hung up.

He could hear all the things Mills hadn't said. Like, why in the hell did you have to pick on my sister for your latest conquest? The situation between Toly and his roping partner was growing more tense all the time.

Wymon's advice to act natural and be himself wasn't winning any points. At this juncture he knew Nikki had to be aware of her brother's attitude toward him. The time for talking to her about Mills's negative feelings was coming soon. This couldn't go on.

NIKKI HAD JUST gotten dressed in jeans and a blouse when her cell phone rang. It was Mills. Curious why he'd be calling her at eight thirty on Saturday morning, she picked up. "Hi! What's going on with my brother?"

"Want a little company?"

She blinked. "Always. Where are you?"

"On my way to your room."

"You're kidding! I'll put the coffee on."

She hung up and opened the door for him before she fixed them their brew. A minute later he walked in and gave her a hug. They sat down in her little sitting room with their mugs. "To what do I owe the pleasure of your company this early in the morning?"

"I thought I'd hang out with my sister while I'm waiting for Toly." Her heart thumped harder just hearing his name.

"Why didn't he come with you?"

Her brother took a long swallow. "He's at the Excalibur having breakfast with a woman he met at the Omaha rodeo. I expect he'll call when he's ready for me to pick him up. I have no clue how long he'll be, if you know what I mean. In the meantime there's no point in waiting for him. Why don't you and I head on over to the center. It'll save you having to bring your own car while we exercise the horses."

Nikki almost choked on her coffee. *Toly was with someone else at this time of morning? Had he spent the night with her?* Pain darted through her so real she felt as if she'd been thrown from her horse and trampled by its hooves.

"Good idea." She forced a smile to hide the hurt. "Are you excited for tonight? I know I am. But I'm wondering which horse I should ride. What do you think?"

He smiled back, something she hadn't seen for a while. "Which one of your three horses will get their feelings hurt the most if you choose the other?"

She chuckled. "I might have known you'd say something like that. I guess I'll have to have a talk with them when we get over to the center and see which of them begs me the most."

Laughter broke from her brother. She hadn't heard that sound for quite a while. Nikki swallowed the last of her coffee. "Turn on the TV if you want while I finish getting ready."

While she was in the bathroom she heard his phone ring. Was it Toly, the cowboy her brother had told her charmed all the ladies on the circuit? The Sapphire Cowboy who'd crept into Nikki's heart without her even realizing it?

Had he told the woman he'd been with all night that she took his breath away? Of course he had, and probably too many other things she couldn't bear to think about. The hurt went too deep.

You have to gird up your loins, her dad used to say when he had a tough task ahead of him. That's what Nikki intended to do.

She put on lipstick and pulled her hair back in a long ponytail. Once she'd fastened it with an elastic, she was ready to face the pain of the day. She ought to be used to it by now because any real happiness didn't last long.

After putting on her cowboy hat, she walked into the sitting room with her purse, pretending she hadn't heard his phone ring. "I'm ready. If Toly should need a ride later, he can reach you at the center, right? Let's go."

Mills turned off the TV. His smile had disappeared. "Actually he did call and is ready to drive with us now."

"Great." She hadn't expected that to happen. They left the hotel for his car. She climbed in the back. "Before we go by for him, do we have time to go to a drive-through for a quickie breakfast?"

"Sure. I'm hungry too."

After they'd made that stop, they pulled up in front of the Excalibur. Nikki was just finishing her burrito when Toly walked up to the car and got in. "Thanks for picking me up."

Mills nodded and they took off.

Toly turned and looked over his shoulder at Nikki who smiled at him.

"We would have brought you breakfast, but I understand you already had it with a girlfriend this morning. Have you been holding out on us?" she teased.

"Not at all," he came back, totally composed. "When we were in Omaha a month ago, we stayed one night at a hotel while I was having the rig serviced. A woman who worked at the hotel and had been to the rodeo asked me to join her for dinner there after our event. I shouldn't have accepted because I wasn't interested and never expected to see her again."

"I couldn't figure out why you did."

Nikki flinched at Mills's comment.

"Because she pushed and I decided to be nice. But it proved to be a mistake. Lyle informed me that she'd sent a lot of emails to our website. I didn't do anything about them until he said she was in Las Vegas. I was surprised to learn she was staying at the Excalibur.

"Lyle actually phoned me about it last night after I'd gone to my rig because she'd sent a bunch more and was becoming a nuisance. So I called the hotel and told her I'd meet her this morning for breakfast because it was all the time I could spare. Mills drove me over there. Once I sat down, I explained that I wasn't interested in a relationship with her, wished her well and left."

Nikki believed him and the relief of knowing the truth made her positively giddy. She couldn't help but wonder why her brother had led her to believe there might be something more to it, leaving it vague. That wasn't nice and it bothered her a lot.

To support Toly she said, "I've had a few guys send too many emails to my blog in the past. You try not to offend anyone, but when they go too far, you have to do something about it. Hey, Mills? Remember that guy from Idaho who turned up at our ranch to see me?"

"Yes," he muttered.

"I don't know how he dared seek me out. Thank goodness Dad was there to threaten him with a law-suit and a shotgun."

Toly's eyes danced as they studied her features. "Did it work?"

"I'll say."

"I wish I'd met your parents."

Her eyes smarted. "So do I."

Mills pulled around the back of the center and got out. He shut his door hard enough that she noticed. When she could get her brother alone, she was going to have a big talk with him. Denise or no Denise, his surliness couldn't be allowed to continue.

Toly walked Nikki inside. On the way to the stalls he grabbed her swinging ponytail and gave it a little tug. She flashed him a sideway glance. Anytime he touched her, she trembled.

"Forgive me. I couldn't resist."

"That I believe. You must have been a rascal when you were little."

His low laugh excited her as they moved to the stalls to put their horses through the paces.

An hour later Nikki dismounted Sassy and hugged her around the neck. "I'm going to ride you tonight and this time we'll get it right." As she was giving all three horses a treat, the guys came by for her and they walked back to the car.

"Mills? Drop me off at the hotel so I can change and get my car." They climbed inside and took off.

"We're having barbecued ribs tonight," Toly reminded her.

Tonight. She couldn't wait. "Those are my favorite. On the way to the RV park I'll pick up the makings for a yummy spinach salad and meet you guys at the rig later."

Toly flashed her a grin. "You and Popeye."

She'd forgotten about Popeye, the famous sailor man cartoon character who ate spinach to make himself strong. "It won't hurt to pack a little iron if we're going to win tonight, right?"

"Amen to that."

But Mills didn't say a word. That did it! She intended to confront him point-blank. He was beyond obnoxious.

A few minutes later he pulled up in front of her hotel. Toly got out and opened the rear door for her.

She thanked him. "See you guys around three."

"I'll be waiting," Toly murmured in an aside.

Her pulse was still racing as she hurried inside to get showered and changed for tonight's event.

Before long she drove her car to the supermarket for the needed ingredients, then headed for the RV park. But instead of going directly to Toly's rig, she walked to the other rig and unlocked the door, calling out to Mills from the entrance.

She could hear his radio playing. Not wanting to walk in on him unannounced when he wasn't expecting her, she phoned him. Pretty soon he answered. "Nikki?"

"Hi. I guess you couldn't hear me come in the rig. Are you decent?"

"Yes."

"We need to talk." She hung up and walked into the kitchen.

Her attractive brother had showered and wandered in wearing a T-shirt and sweats. "What's wrong?"

Nikki sat back in the chair and looked up at him. "Something has been wrong since Denise broke up with you. I've understood that pain, but a new element has been added to the mix that has turned you into someone I don't recognize. Your resentment of Toly since our arrival in Las Vegas has stunned me."

He wouldn't look at her. "What do you mean?"

"You know exactly what I'm saying. You've shown your dislike of him in a dozen ways. This morning you purposely led me to believe Toly had a girlfriend and might have stayed overnight with her. That was dishonest and cruel, both to him and to me. What has Toly ever done to you to make you behave this way?"

His head reared back and his eyes glittered. "So it's true. You've fallen in love with him."

It *was* truth time. "Even if I have, he knows nothing about it."

"The hell he doesn't! You're like all the other women who can't resist the great Toly Clayton. I thought you were different."

She studied him for a minute. "When did your hero worship of him turn to jealousy?"

His hands curled around the chair back. "I'm not jealous. I just don't want to watch him trample over your heart until he gets what he wants and then moves on."

Nikki couldn't believe what she was hearing and jumped to her feet. "Is that what he does? Do you have proof that he's a womanizer who has destroyed lives? He's incredibly attractive, so it's understandable the groupies can't leave him alone, but I've never heard anything like that about him, *except* from you."

Her brother had no comeback. She didn't think so.

"I know there are some cowboys on the rodeo circuit who have developed bad reputations. We girls are aware of the ones to avoid while we're traveling around. To date, Toly's name has never been mentioned except in glowing terms. When he apologized to me that night at the MGM Grand, he admitted that he liked the girls when he first started doing rodeo. But his brother's advice made him wise up fast."

She took a deep breath. "I think you need to analyze what's going on inside of you and decide if you're going to let this anger against Toly rob you of a championship. I love you, Mills, but I don't like what has happened to you. Unless you know Toly has a past prison record or a mistress I don't know about, then I don't want to see you act this way again!" She had the impression he was frightened about something. But what?

Nikki got out of there before she said too much. She had to stop at her car for the groceries before entering Toly's rig. The aroma of the ribs filled the air, making her mouth water.

"Toly?"

"I'll be with you in a minute," he called out from the rear. "Make yourself at home."

It was beginning to feel like she lived there. With Toly in the next room, all was right with her world. She washed her hands and got busy putting the salad together. While she was tossing it with the special avocado dressing, she felt a pair of strong male hands grip her waist from behind and give her a squeeze. A gasp escaped her lips and she almost melted on the spot.

"Sorry if I startled you," he whispered into her hair. Nikki could tell he'd just come from the shower. "I couldn't resist. You have no idea how wonderful you smell."

She could say the same thing to him. What would he do if she turned around and threw her arms around his neck? But before she acted on the impulse, they heard a noise and Mills walked into the kitchen.

Nikki quickly put the salad on the table while Toly took the ribs out of the oven and placed them on the table. That's when she saw him reach for a smaller pan on the lower rack. "You made corn bread? Before Finals are over, you're going to spoil us all rotten."

"That's the idea. I, for one, don't want any of this to end." They sat down at the set table and started to eat.

Neither did Nikki who could only marvel over the food. "I have to amend my judgment of your cooking skills. I don't know how I could have accused you of only knowing how to make coffee when it's clear you could open your own restaurant."

He chuckled and they both ignored the elephant in the room. "I have an idea for tomorrow. Why don't we take the horses out in the desert and ride with no one else around. I think it will be good for all of us to get away for part of a day."

Toly must have been reading her mind. Being around Mills was making them all stir-crazy. "I think that's a fabulous idea."

Of course her brother said nothing. His foul mood hadn't disappeared, but she wasn't going to let him ruin it for her. When she looked at Toly, he flashed her a covert glance.

"I'm glad you said that. We'll stop for fast food on our way back to the center and be there in time for our events."

"Perfect."

"I'm not sure it's a good idea."

Nikki stared at her brother. Here they went again. "Why not?"

"Too much exercise isn't the best thing while we're competing."

She counted to ten. "We'll just walk them. Nothing strenuous. They'll love getting out. So will I."

"I've been thinking about something else," Toly interjected. No doubt he could sense Mills was on the verge of forcing the issue. "What do you say that the day after Finals, we take a helicopter tour of the Grand Canyon before we head home? It only takes four hours and we'll fly over Hoover Dam."

Nikki's heart pounded with sickening speed. *Yes, yes, yes.* She'd done it before as one of the perks when she'd won last year's Miss Rodeo Montana title, but to see it with Toly would be an entirely different story.

"Let's plan on it," she said, so excited about that possibility, she didn't care how her brother was acting. Toly couldn't help but be aware of her brother's continued resentment, but he handled it in a way that made her love him more. He had a maturity anyone would admire.

Once their meal was over, Mills said he was going to his rig to change clothes before they left for the center. *Hooray!*

Nikki watched him go and turned to Toly while she cleared the table. "I'm sorry my brother didn't thank you for dinner. It was fantastic."

"Don't worry about it. We all deal with heartache differently."

"It's no excuse to be rude, especially not to you."

His gaze met hers. "One day he'll get past this."

"Maybe." She loaded the dishwasher. "But will we?"

Toly's laugh filled the interior of the rig and permeated her heart. When it subsided he said, "We *have* to get past it if we want to be number one tonight! My money is on you, Nikki."

"That goes both ways." I love you, Toly. *I love you.*

Chapter Seven

Once they reached the center and parted company, Toly bridled his horse and reached for his Western saddle with its special double rigging. He'd affixed a rubber wrap around the horn to keep the rope dally from slipping when he left the gate.

Checking all the equipment, he saddled Chaz and walked him over to talk to Mills. "So you're going to ride Dusty tonight?"

He jerked his head around. "Yeah. Is that all right with you?"

"I was just making conversation." Toly mounted his horse. "Whatever bad feelings you have about me, can you let go of them long enough while we get through this event? I'll see you at the box."

Tomorrow when he took Nikki riding, he planned to tell her he wanted to be with her all the time. If she felt the same way, then did she have any ideas on how to treat Mills for the next week? He would abide by her decision until they left Las Vegas. After that, he would pursue her because she had fast become the woman he intended to marry. He knew in his soul she was the one.

Toly reached the area to watch as each set of team ropers awaited their turn. When the second-place team got ready, Mills drew up next to him. Soon it was time for them to enter the boxes. Toly was right-handed and walked Chaz in the left one. Mills entered the right box.

The steer had been moved into the chute between them, its horns wrapped for protection. The taut barrier rope ran in front of Toly's box and fastened to an easily released rope on the neck of the steer. It was used to make sure the steer got a head start.

Because he was the header, Toly needed to work with a softer rope that had more elasticity to snag the steer around the horns or the neck. Mills's rope had to be stiffer to rope the hind legs.

As always, Toly said a little prayer for their horses and their safety. These days he included Nikki in his prayer, then called for the steer. But as he was testing his own rope, he experienced that dreaded loss of feeling in his hand and wrist. *Dear God, no.*

A cold sweat broke out on his body. It was too late to do anything about it.

The roar of the crowd was deafening as the assistant opened the chute and the steer ran the length of the barrier rope. Immediately the gate opened and Toly took off, but he couldn't do the wraps of the rope around the saddle horn, called the dally. Without being able to execute that critical move, he couldn't turn Chaz to the left so the steer would follow.

Now that his lower arm had gone slack, the rope rested across his inner elbow. He had to hurl it using the strength from his upper arm and shoulder as the doctor had suggested, and hope it caught a steer horn, one of the three legal catches.

This threw Mills off. He had to make a blind throw, dallying tightly, but Toly couldn't maneuver his horse to face him or the steer. His partner did his best to immobilize it and stretch out its hind legs. But he only nabbed one leg.

When the official waved his flag, Toly's gut told him they'd lost valuable time plus gained a five second penalty because Mills didn't rope both legs. The crowd noise reflected their disappointment. Sure enough their score had been low enough that they probably netted third or fourth place when the scores were averaged. Depending on the scores of the other finalists, their number one standing was now in jeopardy.

In a lightning move he made a grab of the reins with his left hand and turned Chaz around so they could ride out of the arena and down the alley. Once he reached the stall, he dismounted on a run, hiding his right hand under his left arm. Until the feeling came back, he had no strength and it hung lifeless.

He patted his horse's neck. "Sorry, buddy. You did great out there." After signaling one of the attendants to take care of Chaz, he slipped out the back of the center past other contestants getting ready for the bull riding. Toly needed time to recover alone and hurried out to the car. Maybe Mills hadn't seen him leave yet.

He climbed in the backseat and began massaging his lower arm and hand, willing some feeling to come back. His shoulder ached like crazy. For all he knew he'd done some damage there with that throw. This was one time he wouldn't be able to see Nikki perform.

For this to happen in the middle of Finals, it meant a whole new change of tactics. Toly wasn't left-handed, but from now on he was going to have to train using his left hand if they expected to win. Over the years he'd thrown ropes with both hands. But the tricky part had to do with the dally. He needed to work on wrapping it with the hand that wasn't used to doing that maneuver.

It meant no trip to the desert tomorrow. He would train most of the day.

Since they'd planned to pick up fast food afterward, neither he nor Nikki would be cooking tomorrow. No expectations. That was good. While deep in thought, the front driver's door opened. Mills's head appeared. "Toly?"

"Yeah."

"Why didn't you wait for me?" He climbed behind the wheel and looked around at him.

"I…needed to be alone. You go back and watch Nikki."

"Not yet. It's my fault this happened tonight."

Toly's head reared. For once Mills was acting very subdued. "What in the hell are you talking about?"

"It's true. I've been such an ass, I'm surprised you didn't quit on me long before now. I have no right, but I'm going to ask you to forgive me for the way I've carried on about you and Nikki. She called me out earlier." Toly decided his older brother was some kind of a prophet. "I know I've been a jerk, and it put you off your game."

"It's not your fault, Mills. I swear it."

"Nevertheless things are going to change starting right now."

The sincerity in his voice sounded real enough, making Toly feel guilty that he hadn't shared his neuropathy condition with Mills. But he still didn't want him to know the truth until he'd done some training tomorrow. He imagined his doctor would be surprised if he knew what had happened tonight.

If he thought he could get through the rest of the events using his left hand, then he had to find out. Otherwise they would have to withdraw from competition and that would kill Mills. Toly was determined that for his partner's sake, he would move heaven and earth not to let that happen. Nikki's brother deserved and needed to be a national champion.

For the first time in his life, something was more important to Toly than winning. In this last year he'd met the love of his life. Losing the national championship would mean nothing to him personally if he couldn't have a future with Nikki Dobson.

"The only thing important about tonight is for one of us to be there for Nikki. I'll be fine. See you two in a little while. If she wins tonight, you'll have to take her to the South Point to pick up her gold buckle. I'll ask you to drop me off at the RV park on the way. Don't worry. I'll tell her I strained the muscles in my upper arm and shoulder. We don't want her to worry. Now go, or you'll miss her event!"

"We still need to talk, Toly. I've been too protective of her."

"If I had a sister, I'm sure I'd be the same way and probably worse, but we'll hash it out later. Before you go, I want you to know you saved the night with your throw. You got one of the legs, thank heaven, or we'd have ended up with the lowest score of the night and be finished. That's why you're the number one heeler on this year's circuit. Congratulations."

"You managed to snag a horn, Toly. I don't know how you did it. We're still alive."

"Yep. Now get out of here so Nikki will know we're cheering for her."

"I'm going."

After he shut the door, Toly leaned back against the seat. Some feeling had started entering his arm again. The weakness never lasted long, but tonight it cost them. He couldn't allow it to happen again.

Until they returned to the car, he went over the new strategy in his mind. He didn't dare switch boxes with Mills tomorrow night. He'd have to use his left arm to throw and make it work, though it would be harder. He would practice using his left arm before going to the arena.

"Toly?" he heard Nikki call to him some time later before she even opened the front passenger door. Once inside she leaned over the seat to look at him. The fear in her fabulous gray eyes for him was a revelation. It reminded him of the night he'd sought her out at the MGM Grand and she'd been worried about Mills. Things had changed drastically since that night.

"Are you all right? Please don't let one higher score

change anything for you. You'll still average out first because of all your wins."

Could any woman be more beautiful, inside and out? "I'm fine, Nikki. All I need to know is, did you win another gold buckle tonight?"

"She did! You should have seen her sashay around those barrels!" Mills spoke up after opening his door. He sounded elated, but it couldn't match Toly's excitement for her.

Mills started the car and they left for the RV park. Before she could ask, Toly said, "Much as I'd like to see you get your buckle tonight, I've asked your brother to take me to the rig. My shoulder is hurting. I need to put an ice pack on it and get a good night's sleep. That will solve the problem, but I'm afraid it means a ride out on the desert tomorrow is out for me."

"Don't worry about that, Toly. You need to take care of yourself. We'll stay around and make sure you don't starve."

"I don't want you waiting on me. Tomorrow I'll be exercising my horses, but thank you for the thought. Hey, Mills—who did the fastest time tonight?"

"Luis Mondego and Kip Jackson from South Dakota. Clay's team came in second. We were third."

Toly swallowed hard. At least they'd stayed in the top three tonight. There was still a chance for them depending on how well his practice went tomorrow. By late afternoon he would know if he had to tell Mills the bad news or not.

"Thanks for bringing me back first." They'd pulled up to Toly's rig. He got out. His right hand was functioning well enough again that no one could tell what had happened. He stared at Nikki through her open window. "I'd love to go to the hotel tonight. Be assured I'll be there all the rest of the nights."

"Thank you, but I'm not concerned about me." The tremor in her voice got to his heart. "Take care of that shoulder, Toly. We'll see you tomorrow. If you need anything, call no matter the time."

Oh, Nikki. Was he ever going to take her up on that offer when this was all over.

DESPITE HER LATEST WIN, Nikki awakened early Sunday morning, having spent a restless night at her hotel. Toly's hurt shoulder had to have caused him a lot of pain for him to go straight back to the rig. He would never ask for help, but she didn't care. They'd been living in and out of each other's pockets for a while now and she wanted to do what she could for him.

After washing her hair, she got ready for the day and put on the clothes she would wear in her event tonight. Once she'd exercised her horses, she drove to the RV park with some food from a deli she liked. Why not surprise him with a meal? Hopefully his shoulder would be much better.

Nikki didn't see anyone around when she parked her car behind the Dobson rig. She left the food in the car and walked over to the barn to find Toly. Snapper was gone, but Chaz was in his stall. Hmm. She didn't know how long he would be running his horse through the motions.

Finally she walked back to her car and put the food

in the fridge of their trailer while she waited for him. The Christmas tree drew her gaze and she turned on the lights. It added a festive air she loved.

Unfortunately she didn't have Toly's cell phone number, so she called her brother. Mills wouldn't be happy about it, but she was long past worrying about his feelings.

To her disappointment it went through to his voice mail. She left a message for him to call or text her back with Toly's phone number. With her horses stalled at the center, she couldn't ride out to find Toly. Instead she walked to the barn again, hoping he might have come back, but no such luck.

As she wheeled around to leave one more time, he suddenly appeared at the entrance to the stall on foot, pulling the lead on Snapper. A coil of rope hung from the saddle horn. With that sore shoulder, she wondered if he'd been able to get in much practice.

His eyes played over her, making her senses come alive. "I've been thinking about you all day. To find you here couldn't be a better gift."

"I've been hoping you would come back," she said in a breathless voice. "I brought us a meal."

So fast she couldn't believe it, he dropped the lead and drew her into his arms. "Last night I didn't get to congratulate you the way I wanted. For a year I've wanted to kiss you. Now I'm going to do it, ready or not."

"Toly," she whispered his name, melting against his rock-hard body while he covered her mouth with his own. Nikki had never known a feeling like this in her life and came close to fainting from the desire he aroused in her as they began devouring each other. She'd dreamed of being with him, but no dream produced this kind of ecstasy. With his hands roaming over her back and hips, she'd turned wanton, craving his love.

"You're so beautiful, I don't believe you're real." He buried his face in her hair. "I've needed to feel you like this forever."

She twined her arms around his neck. "I wanted you to kiss me while we were dancing."

"Only then?" he teased before kissing each feature of her face. "There were reasons I didn't. Reasons we need to talk about, but right now I can't think."

Once again they gave each other one hungry kiss after another and she felt her passion bursting out of control. She had no idea when they would have come up for air if a couple of riders hadn't come down the aisle and were nearing Snapper's stall.

Toly moaned before easing Nikki away from him. His peridot-colored eyes held a glaze. She could tell he was out of breath too. The people were getting closer. She moved out of Toly's way so he could bring his horse inside the stall.

Once the people had passed, he pressed her against the wall. "Let me take care of Snapper," he murmured against her lips, "then we'll go back to my trailer." He gave her another long, hard kiss.

"I'll help you."

Together they removed the gear and made certain he

had hay and water. Toly's shoulder didn't seem to be bothering him as much now, thank goodness.

"Let's go." He put his arm around her shoulders and they walked back to the rigs. The sensation of their bodies brushing against each other was another new exciting experience she never wanted to end.

"I put the food in our rig. I'll get it and come over to yours."

"That's a good idea. Mills went out with friends a little while ago, but he'll be back soon. Until he gets here I have things to say to you in private."

She felt an urgency coming from him apart from his wanting to be alone with her. What was it about? After retrieving their meal, she took the sack and the Christmas tree to his rig. He'd left the door unlocked. She went inside and locked it again. When she reached the kitchen, she plugged the Christmas lights in, then warmed up the Chinese takeout in his microwave.

He walked in from the other end of the trailer wearing a blue-and-white-plaid shirt. His sensational physique made him look good in anything. "Mmm. All it takes around here is a woman's touch. Christmas and Chinese. It smells delicious."

"I hope you're hungry. I bought a little bit of everything."

"Just the way I like it. How lucky am I to be waited on by a woman like you."

She darted him a sideway glance while she fixed their plates. "What do you mean?" Her curiosity was getting the best of her.

He fixed coffee for them. "Exactly what I said.

There's not another woman like you on the planet. I'm not just talking about your gorgeous looks. Let's face it. No woman compares to you."

Heat swarmed her cheeks. "*Toly—*"

"It's true. But I'm also talking about what you're like on the inside. I've seen how kind you are to the foreman on your ranch, to everyone while you've been on the circuit. The crew thinks you walk on water. I've also witnessed the deep love you have for your brother."

Nikki put their plates on the table and sat down with him. "Brothers are pretty special. You would know all about that." They started eating.

He nodded. "That's why we need to talk about Mills. You're the only person who can advise me what to do."

"If you're talking about his being so r—"

"I'm not." He cut her off gently before she could finish. "This has to do with something much more serious."

"I knew it," she whispered.

"What do you think you know?"

"I'm guessing you've found out why Denise broke up with him."

"No, Nikki. I'm afraid I'm as in the dark about that as the two of you."

She stopped eating. "Now you're making me nervous."

"I don't mean to do that. Just hear me out."

A minute ago he'd said intimate things to her that any woman in love would want to hear from the man she adored. Yet Nikki had the awful premonition he was about to tell her something that was going to turn her world upside down. She wanted to run out of there, but the pained look in his eyes held her spellbound.

"I'm listening."

TOLY HATED WHAT he had to tell Nikki, but she deserved to know the whole truth. He especially hated it that he had to say anything when she had an event tonight and needed all her powers of concentration.

"A month before Denise broke off with Mills, I had an incident while I was training that I didn't tell him or anyone about. Instead I went to our family doctor who referred me to a neurologist in Missoula."

Nikki's gray eyes darkened with what he knew was fear.

"To make a long story short, I have a neuropathy in my lower right arm and hand. It's a nerve that is affected by the tissue around it and causes temporary paralysis. The doctor said that all the years of roping must have aggravated it and that it could come on at any time."

"I just can't believe this would happen to you."

"No one is exempt from the unexpected. Twice during practice in the last two months my hand and lower arm went slack so I couldn't grip the dally. But Mills didn't pick up on it.

"My fear of upsetting your brother was so great, I decided to say nothing and hoped we could get through Finals before it happened again. To my horror, when I was in the block last night testing the rope, my hand and arm went slack. My worst nightmare had happened. It came on so fast I was stunned."

"So that's why you struggled!" Nikki cried. "Oh, Toly—how awful for you." She shook her head.

"But not just for me. For Mills too. If he weren't such an expert heeler, he couldn't have pulled off snagging at least one of the steer's hind legs. Now I have a serious dilemma. After seeing the doctor in the beginning, I could have told your brother everything, but I didn't because I didn't want us to drop out."

"Of course you didn't!"

"We were both going for the championship and the last thing I wanted was to tell him the bad news. He's worked so hard and has been living for this. But I have to be honest. Last night was a moment I'll never forget. I had to call for the steer and see it through, not knowing the outcome. You saw what happened. I had to use all the force of my shoulder and upper arm to throw the rope."

"Then it's a miracle you caught the steer around the horn."

"I agree, and another miracle that Mills was able to rope one of its hind legs to win us a third place and give us a fighting chance."

"How soon did you tell him what happened?"

He stared at her for a few seconds. "I haven't told him anything."

Her eyes searched his. "What does he think went wrong?"

"That I just made a bad toss and hurt my shoulder."

"You *did* hurt it. How does it feel today?"

"It's all right."

Nikki moaned. "No, it's not." She got up from the

table and paced for a minute. "Tell me more about your condition. Can it be fixed?"

"Possibly with surgery, but there's no real guarantee." He didn't want to talk about the disease. Not until the rodeo was over.

She grabbed on to the counter. "So *that's* why you said that once Finals were over, you were giving up the rodeo for good."

"Yes. Otherwise Mills and I could go on the circuit again next season. But as you've gathered, my rodeo days are over. Of course he can team up with another roper going for the championship and enjoy several more years doing it."

"Oh. Toly—" Tears had filled her eyes. "I'm so, so sorry for you."

"Don't be, Nikki. I've had a run most guys only dream of doing. It's your brother I'm concerned about now and that's where you come in."

"What do you mean?"

"For one thing, he feels that my mistake last night was partially his fault because he's been uncommunicative lately. He's afraid it threw me off. You have no idea how guilty that makes me feel because it's not the truth. I told him he was wrong in his supposition and hoped he believed me, but I'm not sure he did.

"That's why I think I should tell him about my condition when he comes back to the rig. He deserves to know the truth. But if he doesn't have faith in me at this point, then we'll be forced to meet with the officials and withdraw before tonight's event."

Her face lost a little color. "To know what's wrong with you and withdraw now would kill him."

"You think I don't know that?" Toly got up from the table and walked over to her, putting his hands on her upper arms. He rubbed them gently. "You're his sister. I'm aware how much you two love each other, so I'm begging you to tell me what I should do."

She put a hand on his chest. "Are these episodes coming more often?"

"Last night was my third one in the last ten weeks."

He heard her take a quick breath. "Are you in pain after one of them?"

Toly loved her so terribly, he couldn't help giving her a brief kiss. "No. It's very strange. Once it's over, you'd never know it had happened or could happen again. There's no warning. Nothing."

"So it's possible you'll be free of them for the rest of the rodeo?"

"Yes. That's what I was banking on while we drove down here from Great Falls in the rig. But he has the right to know that if we go in the arena again tonight, the same thing could happen to me. We might not be so lucky and could end up in last place. That would dash our chances to win the championship."

She closed her eyes in obvious pain.

"Out of desperation, I went out this morning to practice on the dummy using my left arm and hand. The trick is to wrap the dally fast enough, but it's incredibly hard when I haven't done it that way before. Though my left-hand grip is strong, I've never used my left arm for team roping."

"But you *could* do it?" He heard hope in her question.

"Yes. I can try. You must understand it's very iffy. I'd have to race out of the box and hope my effort is good enough to come in with a decent score. So… I have a choice to make."

Nikki's groan revealed her torment.

"Either I tell Mills the truth now and see if he'd rather withdraw or try to beat the odds of another episode coming on during competition. The alternative would be to tell him nothing and I'll bungle through the next seven nights using my left arm, hoping he won't notice."

"He'll eventually find out, don't you think?"

"I don't know. While he's in the arena, he'll be living in the moment so completely that by the time we meet up at the stalls after the event, he won't realize what I did if I get another episode. But if he does notice, then I'll have to come clean. The point is, I can't change midstream. Once I'm in the box, I have to be set. Help me, Nikki," he begged.

Before she could make a sound, her cell phone rang. Nikki pulled it out of her pocket. Toly let go of her and stepped away. She looked up at him. "It's Mills. His timing couldn't be worse. When you weren't here earlier, I went to the barn to find you, but you were out on Snapper. So I called him and left a message for him to get back to me with your phone number."

Toly leaned against the counter. "He's going to want to know why you were asking him for it."

"I'll tell him I brought Chinese food for all of us and couldn't find either one of you."

"That sounds reasonable."

She phoned Mills and put him on speakerphone.

"Nikki? What's going on? Why do you want to speak to Toly?"

"I brought food for all of us and I'm afraid it'll go to waste."

"He's out exercising Snapper and will be back before long. I'm on way to the RV park right now. See you in a minute."

Toly heard the click and she hung up. "He still didn't give you my number."

"No. I'd better unlock the door." She dashed off and came back. "When he walks in, I'll tell him you returned and asked me to bring the food here while you iced your shoulder."

"That explanation ought to work. But before he gets here, I need to know what you want me to tell him."

Nikki grabbed the chair and unconsciously threw her head back, sending her glossy black hair sprawling across her shoulders. "We need the proverbial wisdom of Solomon, you know?"

Everything she said and did enamored him more. "That's why I've put this on you, because I trust you with my life. So does your brother."

Her eyes took on a haunted cast. "You give me far too much credit."

"What pains me most is that you have to carry this burden while you're facing another event tonight. It isn't fair while you're on your way to winning the national barrel racing championship."

He could hear her mind working. "You're honestly willing to try using your left arm?"

"That's why I've spent all day practicing instead of taking you out to the desert for a ride."

She straightened. "Then we can't let your sacrifice go to waste."

He let out the breath he didn't know he was holding. "Thank God you said that."

Toly would have reached for her, but they heard the car pull up. He sat back down at the table and ate one of the jumbo fried shrimps just as Mills walked in the kitchen.

Nikki flicked him a glance. "Come and sit. Toly got here a minute ago and was starving. I bet you are too. Let me serve you." She put a plate in front of him and served everyone coffee.

"Thanks. I love *char siu*."

"I know." He seemed to be in a better mood. She didn't know the reason why, but she was grateful for the slightest improvement.

"How's the shoulder, Toly?"

"Not bad at all."

"That's good. I've been going over the numbers. Last night's third place didn't ruin our standings. Most of the ropings will pay out over two hundred thousand dollars to the team roping winner. Along with your winnings, Nikki, we could really get going on our future ideas for the rodeo."

The shine in Mills's eyes told Toly the right decision had been made to risk everything and stay with the rodeo. His gaze fused with Nikki's. They communed in silence while he promised to do everything in his power to make them come out on top.

Mills finished off the rest of the food, then got to his feet. "I'm going to the rig to change clothes for tonight. Thanks for dinner. See you out at the car in a few minutes."

Toly was surprised he'd left the two of them alone. "While I'm thinking about it, we should have exchanged phone numbers months ago. Let's do it now." She immediately pulled out her phone and they shared numbers to program. He'd wanted to do that forever.

When they'd finished, she started clearing the table while he got up and filled the dishwasher. "Why didn't you just ask me for my number?"

He eyed her directly. "The truth?"

"What do you think?"

"Because once your brother and I decided to hook up, he let me know right away you were off-limits, so I didn't dare go against his wishes."

A delicate frown broke out on her face. "He actually told you that?"

Toly nodded. "But not in those exact words. I figured he was being so protective of you because you'd lost your parents and he was watching out for you. He also told me you were going through a very bad time after breaking up with the man you almost married."

"I can't believe he told you all that. It's embarrassing."

"He loves you. I got the hint and did my best to honor

his wishes. After all, he and I had a mission to get to Finals and I didn't want to upset him by chasing after his beautiful sister. Don't you know you've left a trail of male bodies behind that you could line up around the arena at least a dozen times?"

"That's not true!" She really wasn't aware of her effect on a man.

He laughed. "You'd have to live in my world. I can name a couple of dozen guys who'd like to get to know you and have personally asked for my help because you're Mills's sister. Little do they know they'd have to get past me."

He loved the way she blushed. "You wanted to get to know me?"

"Do you really have to ask me that question? The minute we were introduced, I felt like I was in free fall."

"I don't believe it." But he saw a small smile break the corners of her mouth.

"Lady?" he whispered, afraid Mills might suddenly come back in. "You have no idea of what I've been through trying to get close to you without breaking your brother's set of commandments. Did you never wonder why we trained so much on your ranch?"

"That was your idea?"

"Yes."

"Toly—I wish I'd known."

"Well, you know it now. My mom hasn't been happy about it, I can tell you. She's complained for the last year that she's hardly seen me. It's your fault."

Nikki put away the leftovers while Toly finished filling the dishwasher. There was little to do, which was good. "Why don't we gather our things and go out to the car to wait for him. I want to discuss something with you."

Nikki nodded. Before long they were ready to leave, grabbing their gloves and Stetsons. She unplugged the Christmas tree lights and they hurried out to the car. He helped her in the front passenger side before climbing in the backseat. She turned around to look at him. "What's on your mind?"

"I've been thinking about last night. On a good night it only takes three seconds or less to throw the rope and set up the steer for Mills. If I get in the box while I'm waiting and don't feel that change in my arm and hand before the gate opens, maybe I should go for it with my right arm."

He waited to hear what she would say.

"That's a judgment call only you can make. I believe in you, Toly, and I'll be praying for you." The moment her touching sentiments permeated his being, the other door opened and Mills climbed behind the wheel.

On the way to the center, Toly pondered her words. They reminded him of a seminal moment in his past. He'd been in high school at the time. One weekend after going to the rodeo in Missoula with his dad and brothers, he told them he was going to be a national rodeo champion one day. His father, a former rodeo celebrity, had smiled into his eyes and said those exact words to him.

To think that ten years later, Toly and Mills were

on the cusp of fulfilling that dream. This opportunity would never come for him again.

I have to make it happen for both of us, no matter what.

He looked at Nikki. What would he do if she weren't here believing in him? She'd become his whole world.

Chapter Eight

As soon as they reached the center, the guys took off, leaving Nikki to make her way through the stands to the front where she could watch the team roping event. The place was filled to overflowing every night. As usual the atmosphere of the crowd was electric.

But Nikki felt distanced from everything because she was dying for Toly. Tonight he would have to make a split-second decision once he was in the box. His event would be coming up soon. The pressure on him had to be unimaginable because whatever he did would affect Mills too.

The roar from the steer wrestling event was pretty deafening. But when it came time for the team roping—clearly the fan favorite—everyone was on their feet and the noise was earsplitting.

As the fifteen teams came roaring out of the gates two at a time, she started counting down. Toly's would be third to last. The scores were all over the place from 4.0 to 4.8, but there was only one set she cared about.

"Toly Clayton and Mills Dobson are up next. We'll

see if our top winners coming into Finals can top last night's third-place score."

Nikki could hardly breathe as the steer charged out of the chute. She could see Toly with the rope. It was in his *right* hand. He'd made his decision. "Please, please be all right, Toly."

He shot out of the gate and roped the two horns almost instantly in his ocean wave loop. Mills followed with a superb throw that tied up both hind legs. Their speed and precision caused the audience to thunder their approval and give them a standing ovation. Their time: 3.7 and 3.8. Nikki thought she was going to burst for joy. She heard the announcer say, "No one's going to beat those scores tonight."

No they wouldn't!

As the next team was announced, Nikki hurried through the crowd to the stalls in the back so she could get ready for her event.

Santos wore a huge smile when he saw her coming. "It's a great night, Nikki."

"I'll say it is." He'd been there to get Sassy bridled and saddled. She gave him a hug, but was embarrassed because tears were streaming down her cheeks.

She hugged her horse around the neck. "He did it. He did it," she sobbed.

"Are you all right?"

She turned at Santos's voice and laughed, brushing the moisture from her face. "I'm just so happy."

"We all are. Now let's see you pull another score that will make you even more famous than you already are."

"Keep that bull coming, Santos. I love it." She

mounted her horse, hardly knowing what she was doing. "Come on, Sassy girl. Let's get out there. I want to wow Toly. What do you say?"

Sassy neighed.

Nikki laughed in delight. "Nobody believes you understand me, but I know differently. Tonight is really important."

She passed her competitors and took her place at the end of the line. One by one the girls exploded down the alley. Nikki watched the screen. Several finalists missed their barrels and one took a nasty fall. Sobered by what she'd seen, she drew on her powers of concentration the way Toly had done earlier tonight.

Soon it was her turn. She rode low over Sassy the way she did in practice on the ranch. "Let's do it again," she urged her horse. They sailed around the barrels, cutting them close with no penalties. Then she rode her horse home, praising her all the way. Her time flashed on the scoreboard: 13.39!

"We did it!" she cried to Sassy.

The crowd went ballistic and she heard the announcer say she'd set a record tonight. When she rode to the stall, the guys and crew were there to greet her, but she only had eyes for Toly. His eyes gleamed like gemstones.

She wanted to fall right into his arms, but it was her brother who helped her off her horse and gave her a long hug. "You broke a record, Nikki. Tonight we're going to celebrate the night away."

Nikki hadn't seen Mills in such high spirits since before Denise broke up with him. But all her thoughts were on Toly, who'd fought through his dilemma and his brave gamble had earned them another first-place win. She wanted to show him how she felt, but it would have to wait until they were alone.

They walked out to the car and left the parking area. But her spirits plunged when Toly asked Mills to drive him back to the RV park first. "My arm and shoulder need ice. Do you mind bringing my gold buckle back to the rig after you and Nikki have picked them up? I'd love to be there and honor you two for your brilliant performances, but I need some painkillers."

"That's our number one priority, isn't it, Nikki?"

"Absolutely."

Mills kept talking. "We've got to get you in the same shape you were in tonight. Everything came together like magic for all of us."

"It *was* magic." Toly's comment made her shiver.

"We can do it again, right, Nikki?" Her brother was in high form. She could only hope they had another night like tonight.

But for the moment she wished the situation were different and Toly wanted her with him. Mills could have brought back their buckles while she stayed at the rig with Toly so she could help take care of him. But she didn't have that right. Maybe he preferred to be alone.

Too soon they reached the RV park. Mills pulled up to Toly's rig. After he got out, his glance included both of them. "Go enjoy yourselves and have fun. A night like this is to be treasured. See you guys tomorrow."

"Take care of yourself, bud."

The door closed and they drove back to town. But for

Nikki the rest of the night was a blur and she couldn't wait to get back to her hotel where she could give in to her emotions.

She put her buckle on the dresser with the other buckles. Naturally, part of her was ecstatic about the great scores the three of them had received tonight. But the major part of her needed to give in to the tears she'd been holding back since Toly had told her about his neuropathy.

Before she got ready for bed, she looked up his condition on her laptop, wanting to know all about it. While she was doing some research, her cell phone rang. At eleven at night it could only be her brother, or maybe one of the crew if an emergency had developed. She reached for it and checked the caller ID. The name she saw shocked her to the core.

Denise!

Nikki couldn't believe it and clicked on. "Is it really you?"

"Yes," she said in a halting voice. "I'm surprised you even picked up when you could see I was calling. Y-you have every right to hate me." The stammer told Nikki a lot.

"I could never do that. You've been one of my closest friends."

"Until I ruined everything."

"Whatever you did, I have to believe it was for a very important reason. I'm just surprised you've chosen now to get in touch with me."

"I couldn't put off phoning you any longer. To be truthful, I flew into Las Vegas on the eighth and have been staying at the Mirage Hotel so I could be at the arena every night."

A gasp escaped Nikki's lips. "You've been here the whole time?"

"Yes, and I've watched all the events from a front row seat at the center. Tonight your performance was so spectacular, I wanted to shout to everyone that you were my friend. Honestly, Nikki, I've never been so proud of anyone as I was of you tonight. I caught it all on my phone.

"When I got back to my hotel, I knew I wouldn't be able to go to sleep until I talked to you and let you know how much I've missed you."

Nikki's eyes stung from her tears. A lump had lodged in her throat. Denise hadn't mentioned Mills, but right now she didn't care. It was enough to hear her friend's voice again. "I've missed you too. You'll never know how much I've needed you to confide in."

She could hear sniffling. "Tell me about it. I know you must be exhausted and need your sleep. Would it be possible for us to meet tomorrow morning? I *have* to talk to you, Nikki."

The desperation in her voice convinced Nikki that her friend was going to tell her why she'd broken up with Mills. But Nikki wanted to drive over to Toly's rig as soon as she got up to make sure he was all right before she did anything else.

"Denise? I have an idea. Are you in bed?"

"No."

"Why don't you drive over to the Cyclades Hotel

right now. Bring a bag so you can stay all night in the other bedroom."

"You mean it?" she cried.

"I've been wanting to talk to you too. Let's not put it off any longer."

"I'll come as soon as I can."

Nikki gave her the number of her suite. "I'll be waiting for you."

"You don't know what this means to me."

"I think I do. Nothing's been the same for me since you broke up with my brother."

"Thank you for being the best friend who ever lived."

Nikki heard the click before she hung up.

Talk about a red-letter night…

Tonight Nikki would get answers. She was so excited, she called kitchen services and ordered some club sandwiches and colas to be brought to her room. This would probably last half the night and they would need food.

She closed her laptop and put it in the drawer. Next she changed into her blue sweats to get comfortable. After putting on lipstick and brushing her hair, she heard a knock. "Room service."

Nikki grabbed some cash from her purse and ran to the door to get their dinner tray. Once the waiter was gone, she set it on the coffee table in the sitting room and opened one of the sodas. She didn't have to wait long until she heard another knock on the door. Without hesitation she ran to open it.

There stood her beautiful friend with her long blonde hair and those chocolate-brown eyes that had blown her brother away. "It's so good to see you, Denise!" she cried before they hugged. "Come in."

AFTER AN EARLY Monday morning practice on Snapper, practicing his roping on a dummy, Toly entered his rig and poured himself a cup of coffee. He checked his phone and saw that one of his brothers had called, so he phoned him back.

"Roce?"

"Hey, bro—the way you took down that steer last night left us all breathless. What a score! Congratulations!"

"Thanks." Coming from the brother he'd roped with before Mills had become his partner meant the world to him.

"We all agreed that Dad had to be watching."

His throat constricted. "I'd like to think so."

"Our family expects a repeat performance tonight. Then you'll be halfway there. We're all set to fly out on Saturday."

"I'm looking forward to seeing everyone."

But Toly knew he and Mills wouldn't be duplicating last night's score. Because of his fear over having another episode, he'd overdone it wrapping the dally tightly and had strained his arm. He'd paid the price to get a big win. Tonight he would have to rely on his left arm to do the work.

"Hey—are you all right?"

He gripped the phone tighter. "Couldn't be better."

"That's good. You seem a little subdued."

"I was out practicing before I called you."

"Maybe you're overdoing it. You need to chill for a while."

He sipped his coffee. "That's exactly what I have in mind."

"I have to tell you I'm impressed with Mills."

"He's the best."

"Is he around? I'd like to tell him what a great job he and his knockout sister did out there last night."

Just the mention of Nikki tripled his heartbeat. "Sorry. Mills took off for the center to work with Dusty before tonight's performance. He'll be back later and I'll pass on what you said to both of them. How's Mom?"

"Excited to see you win the championship."

At the moment Toly couldn't imagine getting through six more nights with top scores. "What about your other half?"

"We're happier than I ever thought possible."

"That's great, Roce. Give her and everyone my love. We'll talk again soon."

"Go get 'em tonight, champ!"

No sooner had they hung up than he heard a knock on the door. It couldn't be Mills or he would have just walked in. Maybe it was one of the crew checking in over something to do with the horses. He put down his empty mug and walked through to open it.

"Nikki—"

There she was in all her glory, wearing jeans and a Western blouse her figure did wonders for. Her anxious gray eyes took a detailed inventory of him. "I had to find out how you are. Can I come in?"

"What do *you* think. But first I need this." He pulled

her close with his left arm, shutting the door with his boot. Then he covered her mouth with his own. He found her so delectable, his hunger for her spiraled out of control.

"I'm sorry I got carried away," he whispered against her lips minutes later.

"If you noticed, I wasn't complaining."

He loved this woman and wanted to take her back to his bedroom, never to come out again. "Let's go in the living room where we can be comfortable." He reached for her hand and drew her with him till they reached the couch.

"I think I willed you here," he murmured, pulling her down on his lap. In the process, he forgot about his right arm. The pain caused him to let out a slight groan, but she heard it and moved off him.

"Your arm is bad."

He flashed her a smile. "It's fine if I don't try to do something I shouldn't."

She stared into his eyes. "You overdid it last night."

"You're right, which means I'll be using my left arm tonight. This time I won't have a choice."

"Your performance made history, Toly. It's on all the sports talk shows today. I heard that the betting in Las Vegas is heavy on you and Mills for the overall championship." She gripped his left hand. "When I saw the rope in your right hand and knew what you were going to do, I prayed so hard that horrid weakness wouldn't strike."

"Your prayer reached the right person." He kissed her again, long and slowly before lifting his mouth from hers. "Mills came over early this morning and told me they praised you at the gold buckle ceremony last night. He got you on his phone and let me see his video." He cupped the side of her face. "You deserved every accolade. I'm sorry I couldn't be there."

She kissed his jaw. "I'm glad you were here taking care of yourself. That's all that matters to me. Let me get the ice pack for you."

"I'll apply it later if I need it."

"If you're sure. How about some more painkillers?"

"Not yet."

"Do you want me to fix you something to eat?"

"I won't be hungry for another hour. Now tell me what's going on with you."

"What do you mean?"

"We've been together a lot lately and I sense you've got something on your mind."

She averted her eyes. "You must be psychic."

"I wouldn't go that far." He kissed her again. "But I want to know what it is before I die of curiosity. Remember we have another event tonight. I'd like to be there."

A gentle laugh escaped. Then she quieted down. "Denise called me last night."

Denise?

Unbelievable.

He pulled her close with his left arm. "That *is* news. Tell me everything."

"She's been in Las Vegas since the eighth and has come to the center every night. I couldn't believe it."

"Where's she staying?"

"At the Mirage. When I found that out, I asked her to drive over to my hotel and spend the night. It was so wonderful to see her again. I'm afraid we talked until three in the morning."

He played with her gorgeous black hair. "That must have been some conversation."

"It was." Nikki turned so she could look at him. He saw those heavenly eyes fill with moisture. "She never wanted to hurt Mills. She's terribly in love with him. It's the kind that will never go away."

He cocked his head. "But?"

"The day before she broke up with him, she came home from work and discovered she had a visitor at her door. It was Johnny Rayburn, the guy she'd known long before she ever met Mills. They'd met in college and dated. She didn't know until he'd asked her to marry him that he'd signed up to go in the military and make it his career.

"Though she loved him, that news came as a shock. It was the last life she wanted. I'm afraid Denise is a lot like me. We're both homebodies and love our ranch life. She couldn't handle the thought of living in other parts of the world as a soldier's wife, of being away from her family and her horses. She knew it wouldn't work and ended their relationship."

Toly frowned. "Did Mills know all about this?"

"Of course. She didn't meet my brother until two years later. If you recall, they were crazy about each other from the first moment they met."

He nodded. "I remember."

Nikki took a deep breath. "She never thought she'd

see Johnny again. But there he was on her doorstep five weeks ago, out of uniform with a prosthetic where his hand had been."

Whoa.

"Johnny told her he was working at his father's insurance firm and found out she wasn't married. He admitted he was still in love with her and hoped that now he was home and out of the military for good, she would consider going out with him again."

"Good grief." Toly got up from the couch.

"Good grief is right," Nikki said. "As you can imagine, Denise was torn apart to see what had happened to Johnny. But she was in love with Mills and didn't have those kinds of feelings for Johnny anymore. Naturally, to see him like that broke her heart.

"He asked her to go out with him so they could talk. When she explained that she was in love with someone else, he asked if she was engaged to this other man, if she was planning to marry him. That put Denise on the spot because Mills had never discussed marriage with her. She told him no, but hoped it would happen in the future."

Toly rubbed the back of his neck. "So Johnny figured all was fair and he prevailed on her, knowing she'd loved him once and would feel sorry for him. He wanted a fighting chance now that he was home and not going anywhere."

"Yes." Nikki flashed him a glance. "Like I said. You're psychic."

"No. I was just putting myself in that poor dude's place. I'm not sure I wouldn't have done the same thing under those circumstances. Knowing the way Mills feels about her, it's not hard to understand why this wounded veteran would want to win back the woman he'd loved."

"Denise *is* a wonderful person. Of course she had no intention of getting back together with Johnny, but she felt she needed to tread carefully and find a way to let him down. She sensed Johnny was fragile. When he told her he had PTSD and was getting therapy, that did it for her.

"Since Mills was so caught up facing Finals, she thought it might be better if he didn't have to worry about her. In the end she decided to stop seeing him until she got through to Johnny without hurting him too badly."

Toly shook his head. "I still don't understand that kind of thinking, but maybe it's because I'm not a woman. To me it's so simple. Just tell Mills what she was doing—he would have understood."

"Maybe. But she wasn't as secure with Mills because he'd never discussed a future with her."

"Not in all the time they'd been dating?"

"No. It's his insecurity. Denise's fears were real. What if he didn't have marriage in mind with her? What if she'd told him everything and he'd started fearing that maybe she was still in love with Johnny deep down? What if the news threw him off enough to affect his performance?"

"That's crazy, Nikki. How could she not have realized how adversely it would affect him by ending it with him and offering no explanation?"

"But he didn't give her enough to go on."

Toly shook his head. "I'm trying to understand."

"So am I. Since she knew she needed time to make Johnny realize he needed to move on with his life, she thought it would be better if Mills didn't know anything about it until you two had gone through Finals. She admits now it was probably the wrong thing to do and regrets it with all her heart."

"I take it Johnny hasn't given up."

"No." Nikki got to her feet. "Denise finally found the courage to end it with him. Since she'd already blocked out her vacation time at work, she flew to Las Vegas to watch Mills and be here when it was all over so they could talk. Denise loves him so much, Toly, and she's in torment."

"Has she asked you to intercede?"

"No. Not at all. She called me because we're friends and she wanted me to know the truth. As for Johnny, she can only hope that one day he'll realize he needs to find someone else to love."

"Do you *want* to do something about it?"

"I don't dare. If I told Mills the truth now, his first reaction would be one of anger. I'm afraid this has to be worked out between the two of them after Finals are over. What I don't understand is why my brother has never told her he wants to marry her."

"Probably because having worked with him all year, I've discovered he wants more money in the bank and his ducks all lined up when he proposes. Your dad was a great role model, you know."

"But she doesn't care about that!"

"Haven't you noticed he has a more protective side to his nature since the death of your parents?"

She nodded. "It's all so complicated when it didn't need to be."

"I couldn't agree more. But we have to face the fact that she has hurt him, even if it was for the best of reasons."

"You're right."

He studied her features for a moment. "Why don't you and I go out for lunch at a drive-through? You'll have to take us since you have the only car."

Her face lit up in a smile. "I was just going to suggest it. Do you think you should take a pain pill first?"

"No. I'm okay as long as I don't wrap both my arms around you the way I want to. But I'll need another kiss before we go anywhere. Come here to me, you gorgeous creature."

"Toly—"

Holding and kissing her had become an addiction. The last thing he cared about was food or anything else. Nikki had become his whole world. After mocking his brothers who caved after meeting the right women, he now understood. But he needed to get her out of there, and tore his lips from hers before he forgot everything else.

"Come on." He gripped her hand and they headed outside to her car.

"How did it go wrapping the dally with your left hand this morning?" she asked while driving them to Buck's Fast Food for hamburgers and shakes.

"Not that great."

"But you'll do it well enough to stay on top. I know you will."

"Your faith in me is humbling."

"You had to be in the stands and watch what you did last night to convince me you can do anything. I wish there was something I could do to help."

"With you championing me, I don't want for anything else."

"Liar," she teased. "I think it's time to get you back to the rig. Your eyelids are getting heavy so I'm going to drop you off after we get our grub, and leave you to get a good nap with some ice and a pill. Hopefully you'll be revived for tonight. For once I'm going to drive to the center and meet you there."

What he wanted was to nap with her. But both of them knew it wouldn't be a good idea whether Mills was around or not.

When they returned to the rig, he leaned toward her. "Thanks for lunch, but most of all for your company. I needed you today, Nikki. You'll never know how much." He cupped her neck so he could give her a thorough kiss. "You're going to get another first tonight. I can feel it in my bones. Drive carefully and I'll see you later."

"I can hardly bear to leave you, Toly," she said and wrapped her arms around his neck to kiss him again. "Promise me you'll stay safe."

The throb in her voice was like music to his ears.

Chapter Nine

Toly got out of the car and waved her off. A minute later Mills walked inside the rig. "I passed Nikki on the way in."

"She came by and took me to Buck's. We would have brought a burger back for you, but didn't know when we'd see you."

"Don't worry about that. How are you doing?"

"Good." He took another pain pill and pulled the ice bag out of the fridge. "I'm going to baby my arm until we leave for the center. Nikki says she'll meet us there."

"Hmm. That's a first for her. I would have thought she'd cook up a storm today."

He followed Toly to his bedroom where he lay down on top of the mattress. "She might have, but I told her not to bother because I'm going to sleep for a while."

"Good idea. Can I get you anything else?"

"No, thanks. How did your practice go?"

"I exercised both horses. I think I'll ride Dusty again."

"They're both winners. You can't go wrong."

"Wouldn't it be great if we could pull the same score tonight?"

Toly closed his eyes. "It would be miraculous."

"I know, but you can't help a guy from dreaming."

"Nope."

"You're obviously tired. I'll go over to my rig and phone you when it's time to leave for the center."

"I'd appreciate that."

After his partner left, he rearranged his pillows to get more comfortable, but nothing could take away his guilt for not telling him about Denise. The woman Mills loved would be out in the crowd tonight watching him.

Toly went through the conversation with Nikki in his mind and decided she'd been right. This was a situation only Mills and Denise could solve. Right now Toly had his own crisis to get through. He'd done the figures in his head. If they got a third place tonight, they were still in contention for a first place overall. That is if Shay didn't do something extraordinary, which he could.

But during the rest of the nights they would have to get some seconds and firsts. If he rested his right arm for three more events, then the last two nights he would use it again. Of course that depended on his not having another episode. Toly never knew when they would come. He was living with a virtual time bomb and his poor partner knew nothing about it.

Here Toly was questioning Denise's judgment when his own was in question. Why didn't he tell Mills about his neuropathy? Nikki didn't think it was wise to tell him, either. So one way or another, all three of them were guilty of keeping Mills in the dark.

Toly tried to put himself in his partner's shoes, but that didn't work. At one point he dozed off, and then his cell phone rang. When he looked at his watch, he couldn't believe it was time to leave for the center.

In a few minutes he'd changed clothes. After grabbing his gloves and hat, he joined Mills at the car. They took off and his partner chatted all the way about scores and what they had to do. Toly knew exactly what they had to do. He needed his left arm and hand to deliver a score that rated in the top three of the night.

To his disappointment he didn't see Nikki at the stalls. She was probably with Denise. Mills was surprised because his sister had always been there to cheer him on.

They walked to their stalls and got ready for their event. Andy had already prepared their horses. All Toly had to do was mount Snapper. When they were ready, they rode to the boxes to wait for their turn.

There'd only been two times in his life Toly had known real fear. One was when his father had been accidentally shot. The other was the night he heard Wymon had been kidnapped and almost killed. Tonight represented a third time that also involved a life-and-death situation.

But the stakes were different. As much as Toly would love to win the championship, he knew his partner needed it more. Everything in Mills's life depended on it. The Dobson twins didn't have family supporting them; their parents were gone. They needed money to keep the ranch going. They both could stand to revel in that moment of glory, vindicating all those years of hard work and dedication to the sport they loved.

Toly gripped the reins with his right hand and walked Snapper into the box. The steer between him and Mills was a wily one, anxious to get out. Toly flicked his partner a glance and knew the exact moment Mills saw he was going out there to rope with his left arm.

His body went cold because Mills would have figured out Toly's right arm couldn't do the job. Hell and hell.

It was time to call for the steer.

The chute opened. Toly had never prayed so hard in his life. He raced after the steer, roping him around the head, and then he wrapped the dally as hard and fast as he could to turn it. Mills roped those hind legs on cue and they left the arena with a 4.0, 4.2 score and hoped it meant a decent ranking.

They rode back to the stalls and dismounted. Mills eventually walked over to him. "I didn't realize your right arm was hurting so badly."

"Sorry I couldn't pull through for us tonight. I'm hoping I'll be able to use it tomorrow night."

"Santos said we came in second. We've still held on to our first-place average."

No thanks to Toly. "That's the best news tonight. You were sensational out there, Mills. Come on. Let's go watch Nikki knock them dead."

Not only was Toly madly in love, he was so proud of her he didn't know how to contain it. Earlier this evening she'd kissed the daylights out of him. A man could die for a kiss like that, but he was shockingly alive and ready for more.

NIKKI AND DENISE hugged each other the moment the announcer came over the loudspeaker proclaiming that Toly and her brother still held the overall lead.

"I'll call you when I'm back in my room and let you know the way is clear so you can come over again."

"Can't wait. Good luck out there, Nikki. There's no one who can touch you."

"Oh, yes there is, but thanks for being my friend."

Taking her leave, she hurried through the stands to the stalls where Santos waited for her with Bombshell. He gave her the thumbs-up when she mounted her horse. "All bets are on you, Nikki."

"Thanks, Santos. That means everything."

She left the stall and walked her horse along the aisle. Five more nights and she would never go through this glorious experience again with Toly. Whatever the future held, she would treasure this moment forever.

While the finalists were gathering, she chatted with a few of them on her way to the end of the line. Tension was building. Nikki could feel it with the girls. They all wanted to win the championship. No one wanted it more than she did, but she wanted the guys to come out on top too. The three of them were in this together.

Nikki leaned forward to pat her horse's neck. "Remember how we went around the practice barrels this afternoon? Let's do it again."

Close to her turn now, the adrenaline surged through her veins, giving her a sense of empowerment. It was heady stuff.

"Up next is Nikki Dobson of the Sweet Clover Ranch in Great Falls, Montana. This rodeo queen has gained the lead. Let's see what she can do tonight on Bomb-shell!"

Her smart horse knew what to do, opening up her stride to enter the arena. After slowing her down around the first barrel with her inside rein, Nikki raised both to give Bombshell the freedom to accelerate in a straight line for the second barrel.

She entered the pocket in an arc and then headed for the third barrel. This one was always tricky. Nikki knew to pick up Bombshell's shoulder using her rein and leg. Once she'd moved her over and collected at the same time, she could finish with a tight turn and run home with power.

The roar from the audience was electric as she rode out of the arena with a 13.60, almost as good as last night. Once again her prayers had been answered. This time when she rode to her stall it was Toly, not her brother, who helped her down with his left arm and gave her a hug.

"I've decided you're a new kind of superhero," he whispered. "You're blowing the place up."

"I think you already did that a little while ago," she whispered back. If there was such a state of too much happiness, this was it.

"Way to go." Mills gave her a huge hug while Santos took care of her horse. "Let's go celebrate."

Mindful of Toly's sore arm, she looked up at him. "Why don't you guys call it a night and take care of that sore arm." They wouldn't be getting gold buckles tonight. "I'll go to the South Point and then I'll drive on back to the hotel. I really am bushed."

Mills frowned. "You don't want me there?"

"Of course, but maybe Toly will need some waiting on, and I'll only be at the South Point long enough to pick up my buckle. We'll have our own celebration tomorrow when I drive out to fix you guys waffles and sausage. How's that?"

Toly flashed her a heart-stopping grin. "That sounds perfect to me."

She knew he was hurting. "Good. Then it's a date."

Without hesitation she took off for her car, not wanting to get detained by Mills. He could tell something was going on. He had radar like Toly's. She decided it was a team roper thing because they'd had to work in harmony for so long.

An hour later she left the South Point having collected her buckle and pulled out her phone to call Denise. "I'll be at the Cyclades in a few minutes. Come over as soon as you can. I'll leave the door open."

"Thanks. You did it again tonight, Nikki. You really are on your way to the championship. I get gooseflesh just thinking about it."

So did Nikki.

ON TUESDAY MORNING the guys were so hungry, Nikki made another batch of waffles. She was relieved to see Toly had a good appetite and looked rested. She'd bought fresh strawberries from the market on her way over to his rig. They disappeared along with the sausage.

Mills poured more coffee for them. "Are you going to ride Bombshell again tonight?"

"No. She needs a rest. Sassy is ready for another go. I'm going to set up the practice barrels and work with her later today. What about you?"

"Dusty's doing great. I'll stick with him tonight. What about you, Toly?"

"I'll ride Snapper again."

Nikki eyed him. "How's the pain this morning?"

"Not nearly as bad as yesterday."

"That's wonderful, but, more than ever, you need to rest that arm. After I've gone over to the center to practice, I'll come back with dinner before we leave for tonight's events."

"You're spoiling us rotten." She caught Toly's smile just as his phone rang. When he answered, she could tell it was his family calling. She got up to clear the table and get the dishes done. The lighted Christmas tree reminded her that her favorite holiday was coming up soon. Once Finals were over she had a lot of shopping to do.

Denise planned to go with her while they were still in Las Vegas. Both of them wanted to find the perfect gifts for the men they loved. Since it appeared his family wanted to talk ranch business and would be on the phone awhile, she waved goodbye to Mills and left the rig.

He surprised her by following her out to her car. "Before you leave, there's something I want to talk to you about."

Her pulse quickened. Could he have possibly found out that Denise was there? She knew Toly wouldn't have told him.

"What is it?"

"Something's different about Toly."

Uh-oh. "Really?" She got in the driver's seat, but that didn't deter Mills.

He climbed in the front passenger side and shut the door. "I don't think he's telling me everything about his arm. What do you know that I don't?"

Heat warmed her cheeks. "Why are you asking me that?"

"Because I can tell you're really worried about him."

"No more than I would be about you."

"Come on, Nikki. It's me you're talking to. Night before last my heart went to my throat when I saw the way he threw the rope. Last night I could hardly breathe when I saw him use his left arm. He's never trained with it. But I can't get him to talk to me about it. I know *you* know the truth and I'm not letting you drive away until you level with me."

Nikki shuddered, realizing she had to put him out of his misery. Otherwise he wouldn't be able to perform at his best for the rest of the rodeo. But when she told him the truth, she feared he would feel so badly about Toly, it would affect him in a worse way.

What to do…

Forgive me, Toly. My brother needs an explanation.

She turned to face him. "All right. I'll tell you the truth." For the next little while Nikki told him about Toly's neuropathy. "He's had three episodes since he was diagnosed. Two happened during practice before you drove to Las Vegas. But the third one came on when he was in the box two nights ago."

Mills shook his head, but he'd lowered it so she couldn't see his expression.

"He's been going through excruciating torment to keep the news from you because he wants you guys to win the national championship. He feared that if he told you, it might make you want to pull out, which was the last thing he wanted. Yesterday he practiced throwing the rope with his left arm and it paid off because you got a second place last night."

Silence followed her comments.

"When did he tell you?" he finally asked in a deceptively quiet voice.

"The afternoon I brought the Chinese food for you. He said he needed my advice about something. I had no idea. When I learned about his condition, you can't imagine how heartbroken I was, not only for him but for you!"

"Did he swear you to secrecy?"

"No. It wasn't like that. Toly was torn apart and wanted me to tell him if he should tell you the truth, knowing you might decide to withdraw from the competition. He said he would abide by my decision because he trusted me with his life. Toly also said that he knew you trusted me more than anyone else in the world."

Mills lifted his dark head. "So *you* influenced him not to tell me?"

"After he told me he would start training with his left arm in order to stay in the competition, I knew in my heart and soul he didn't want to give up. I didn't want him to give up, either, so that's why he didn't tell you."

A grimace marred her brother's good-looking features. "I see. Interesting, isn't it, that he couldn't tell me, the guy he asked to partner with him for an entire year? We would have talked it over and discussed strategies. Instead, he decided I would have just given up everything we'd worked for because he had no faith in me."

"Yes, he does—" she cried, but he wasn't listening.

"No, Nikki. He came to you." She felt him trembling. "I find that the worst form of betrayal. When I get out of the car, I'm going back to his rig to tell him he can go to hell."

"Mills—you don't mean that. I know you're angry. But please, please be angry with me, not him. He was ready to be honest with you. I'm the one who made the final decision."

"Which means you have no faith in me."

By now *she* was trembling in frustration. "You're wrong, Mills. As Mom and Dad told me many times, you were born with an exceptionally compassionate nature and a pure heart."

"That's bull."

"You know it isn't because they told you that to your face when you didn't want our dog to be put down. I was there, remember?"

He lowered his head.

"I can point out dozens of other times too, especially after our parents died. You were there for me, comforting me like a guardian angel. I happen to know it's a fact that if Toly had come right out and told you what was wrong, you would have been totally heartbroken for him."

A strange sound escaped his lips.

"Don't shake your head. I know you, Mills. You would have put his welfare and pain above yours and let go of your dream to win a championship because you're selfless."

She could tell he was restless and ready to get out of the car. Nikki had to make one last attempt to reach him.

"Toly recognizes those traits in you. Have you forgotten he could have chosen any heeler in the country to work with him on this year's circuit? To think that he asked you to be his partner should tell you how much he respects and admires you, not just your horsemanship. Promise me you'll consider everything I've said before you tell him to go to hell."

Nikki's words resonated in the interior of the car before he got out. At least he didn't slam the door. Hopefully that meant something. This was a new situation for all of them. If she'd made matters worse, she guessed she'd find out soon enough.

As much as she'd have liked to warn Toly with a phone call, she didn't dare in case Mills had already gone in the rig to confront him. He'd know in a second if she was on the phone to him. But she could send him a text before she turned on the engine and drove away.

TOLY HAD JUST gotten off the phone after talking ranch business with his brother Eli, when he saw that Nikki had just texted him. He'd hoped that she would have stayed with him. But she had another event tonight and no doubt wanted to get in some practice before she came back with their meal. He checked to see what she'd sent.

Sorry. Mills knows about your neuropathy. My fault.

No sooner had he taken a deep breath than he heard the distinctive knock on the door.

"Come on in!"

Mills walked through to the kitchen.

Toly eyed him over his coffee cup. "What are you doing back here? I thought you were headed for the center."

When Mills was upset, his hard jaw gave him a fierce look. He was loaded for bear. Apparently he'd suspected something wasn't right and had broken Nikki down. Toly wasn't sorry. It was time he knew the truth.

"When were you going to tell me about your disease?"

"Only one person besides my doctor knows about it, so I take it Nikki has told you everything."

"You're damn right. Thanks for trusting the guy you've been training and competing with for the last year. You're some friend, Toly Clayton."

"For just a minute, would you try to put yourself in my place?"

"No, Toly. That argument doesn't hold water. This issue goes far beyond winning the rodeo. I thought we were closer than friends." The pain Toly could hear in Mills's voice cut him like shards of glass. "You know. Brothers."

He swallowed hard. "That's the way I've felt about you for a long time."

"The hell you have! I don't think you know the meaning of the word." His gray eyes looked suspiciously bright. "Funny, isn't it, that all this time I was worried you would break Nikki's heart because you couldn't settle on one woman, and you've done an almighty job of breaking mine."

Toly knew there was no reasoning with him right now. Maybe Mills would never be able to get over it or forgive him. To try to make things better would be futile until he'd had time to absorb what he'd learned. All Toly knew at this point was that Mills wasn't the only one with a broken heart.

"Damn you, Toly," his voice grated before he flew out of the rig, slamming the door behind him.

A groan came out of Toly. There wasn't anything he could do. In Mills's state, no one could know where he'd gone or how he would deal with his pain. Toly didn't suppose even Nikki knew how to solve this one. Not yet anyway.

Before he did anything else, he sent her a text.

Mills delivered his message and hit his target dead center. He's not in good shape, but I'm thankful he heard it from you, the one person he loves and knows he can count on. I'm living till I see you this afternoon. T.

On his way out the door to do some practice throws on the dummy steer, he saw the car and was surprised.

That meant Mills could be in his rig, or exercising Dusty in the RV park arena, or had even gone for a run.

No matter what, right now Toly needed to carry out his routine for today. His right arm was still too sore to use tonight. Tomorrow night it ought to be okay, but then he had to worry if his condition would act up on him at the wrong moment. This was agony.

Once he reached the barn, he grabbed the rope he needed and walked out in back to throw loops with his left hand. He didn't see any sign of Mills. An hour later he went back to the rig, popped some painkillers and took another nap.

When he awakened he saw that Lyle had left him a text congratulating him on their wins. He also asked him to take a look at the email he'd sent him. Amanda Fleming had made a post on the blog that Toly ought to see.

His anger flared. Amanda again?

Toly put the laptop on the kitchen table and opened the message.

For all you fans, I have news. Toly Clayton is a two-faced jerk. I ought to know. After being with me a month ago, the creep only had ten minutes for a cup of coffee after I traveled all the way to Las Vegas to be with him. I wonder how many women have ended up being dumped by him after loading them with promises. Is it because Nikki Dobson has him hog-tied? They show up together every night at the South Point. Does she know what he's been doing out on the circuit when he's on his own? Wouldn't she be shocked to know what he was doing with me?

I know a lot of people would like to know my story. In fact, I know a number of magazines that would pay a lot of money for an exclusive from me with the reigning cowboy in Las Vegas. I even have pictures.

Toly didn't give her post two thoughts before he picked up his phone and called Lyle.

"You've read it?"

"Yes. If I weren't leaving the rodeo forever, I'd hire an attorney and sue her for slander. But she's not worth the trouble. By the weekend my career will be over and the website will no longer be online. She'll have to pick on some other dude and rant elsewhere."

"What?"

"Yep. But don't tell a soul, and don't count out Mills who has several years yet and will hook up with another header."

"But, Toly—"

"That's my exclusive, Lyle," he interrupted him. "I'll call you again this weekend and you can go rogue with it once I'm back in Montana on the ranch."

"You're really giving it up?"

"I am. Thanks for all you've done. I'll be in touch soon."

"Wow. I can't believe it."

"You want to know what I can't believe? That someone like Ms. Fleming is that desperate for attention. I can almost feel sorry for her. Isn't it sad how many of them are out there?"

He hung up the phone. This had been Toly's lucky day with Amanda lining up behind Mills. Just wait until tonight when Toly's left arm let him down. The only light he could see in his life was Nikki. Where in heaven was she?

Chapter Ten

"Knock, Knock!"

Nikki—

Toly hurried over to the door to let her in. Her arms were loaded with their dinner, but all he could see were her pain-filled eyes above the sacks. She walked through to the kitchen and put them down on the counter. He was right there to pull her into his arms and they clung to each other.

"Forgive me for telling him, Toly."

He covered her face with kisses. "Mills had to be told."

"I wouldn't have, but when he followed me out to the car earlier, he'd figured out that something was going on and demanded to know what it was. I couldn't hold back any longer."

"Shh," he murmured, sealing her words with another long, hungry kiss. "If I made a mistake by not telling him immediately, it's too late now."

"You and I made it together, Toly. If I know my brother, this won't cause him to give up even if right now he wants to. Come on. Let's eat before we have to drive over to the center."

She was his rock. He held her for a moment longer before lifting his head. "Something smells good."

"I picked up meat pies with potatoes and gravy at the deli." She eased away and emptied the sacks. "Here's some mint brownies for an hors d'oeuvre if you need one right now." She put their food on the table and they sat down.

"How did you know I've been craving one?"

Nikki grinned. "I'm psychic when it comes to your appetite." Her glance fell on the open laptop. "More fan mail?"

"It's a post Lyle sent to me from an ex-fan."

"Uh-oh. Do I dare read it?"

"Only if you want to."

"I'm glad I got rid of my website," Nikki said before settling down to look at it. She read a couple of lines. "This is the woman you had coffee with the other morning."

"The very one."

"Ooh. She's mad." Nikki scrolled further. "There's nothing about the rodeo here."

Their eyes met. His held amusement. "Of course not."

She ended up reading the whole thing. "Surely this groupie knows you could go after her with a lawsuit, but she's probably disappeared already and you'd never find her."

Toly ruffled his dark blond head unconsciously. "I'd never want to." She loved it when he mussed it. The man was so striking, it didn't surprise her he'd received a post like that one on his blog. No one could match Toly.

He shut the laptop and leaned over to give her a deep kiss. "Mmm. You taste like mint."

Nikki chuckled. "So do you. How's your arm?"

"It's not too sore right now."

"Thank goodness."

They dug into their Chinese food. She kept hoping Mills might get in touch with her. But after knowing about his conversation with Toly, the news had enlarged the pit in her stomach. At the end of their meal her phone rang. She checked the caller ID before flicking him a glance.

"It's Mills." She picked up and put it on speaker. "Hey—where are you?" She was holding her breath.

"I'm at the center and will see you there."

"Great." She heard the click before she could say anything else.

Toly stared at her. "At least he's planning to compete tonight."

"Yes. I *know* he's going to get over this. We just have to give him more time and believe he'll move past this."

He shook his head. "I wish I had your faith. I couldn't have inflicted more damage if I'd shot him in the back. This on top of Denise's rejection is as bad as it gets."

She cleared the table. "Maybe the anger beneath these tumultuous feelings will help him get through the rest of the competition."

"That's one interesting way of looking at it." He put his left arm around her waist and drew her against his body. "Thank God you're here, Nikki," he spoke into her hair. "I couldn't get through this without you."

Nikki's hands slid up his chest to cup his chiseled face. "I feel the same way. We're in this together, and we'll see it through." For the first time since coming to Las Vegas, she took the initiative and kissed him with all the longing that had built up inside of her. Their bodies tried to merge.

His hungry response robbed her of breath. "I need you, Nikki Dobson," he said in a husky voice. "I wish to heaven we didn't have to leave for the center."

"But we do," she half moaned the words and eased away. "I'll finish the dishes when I bring you back later. Gather your things and we'll go."

On the drive to the center, Nikki felt that somewhere along the way they'd charted a new course. He might be a team roper, but the header and the barrel racer had become a team, bound by invisible cords over their love for Mills and all that this grueling year of hard work and sacrifice represented.

Nikki pulled in back of the center and they made their way to the stalls. One of the events had started and the noise of the crowd was unreal. Andy had Snapper bridled and saddled. "Mills said to tell you he'd meet you in the alley."

"Thanks, Andy. You and Santos do great work."

But beneath his Stetson, Toly flashed her a worried, silent message that tugged on her emotions. "It'll be fine," she whispered. "God bless you tonight."

"I already asked Him to bless you."

"Toly." Her voice caught.

He led Snapper out of the stall and mounted him. There was no more magnificent sight than Toly astride his horse dressed in his black Western shirt and jeans, the epitome of male beauty.

After he disappeared, she made her way through the stands to the place where Denise was waiting for her and they hugged. It meant everything that the woman who'd become her dear friend was here to talk to.

Last night she'd confided in Denise about Toly's condition. "Unfortunately today I had to tell Mills about Toly's neuropathy. He knew something was wrong. Toly and I had agreed not to tell him until the rodeo was over, but it didn't work out that way."

"Oh no—"

"It was horrible. He felt completely betrayed and looked like he'd lost his best friend. In a way it was almost as bad as the way he looked when he told me you'd broken up with him. My brother can't take much more. Neither can Toly," she whispered. "He's been living a nightmare since that episode the other night."

Suddenly the team roping was announced. They looked at each other without having to say a word. A bad night tonight could cause the guys to slip from their first-place standing and there'd be no coming back from it.

One by one the teams raced out of their gates, racking up a lot of times between 4.6 and 4.4, but as the announcer said, "The time to beat is 4.2. Here come our first-place winners from Montana, Toly Clayton and Mills Dobson! Can they do it again?" The crowd went crazy with everyone on their feet.

"I'm going to jump out of my skin."

Nikki looked at her friend. "You're not the only one." With her eyes glued to the box, she waited for them to race out. *Come on, Toly. You can do it, you can do it.*

Suddenly the gates lifted and he exploded into the arena. Nikki watched in wonder as he threw a perfect loop with his left arm that caught the steer around the horns. Mills snagged its legs in one swift throw. It all happened so fast and was over before she could take another breath.

Denise grabbed her and they both broke down in tears. "They got a 4.0 and 4.2. They did it!"

Another miracle for Toly.

Nikki sent up a prayer of thanksgiving that her brother had channeled his anger and hurt in a way that got them through another night. If they kept this up, they were on track to win it all.

"Oh boy. Now it's my turn."

"I'm not worried about you, Nikki."

She turned to Denise. "You don't know how glad I am that you're here. I'll call you tonight when I get back to the hotel. See you later."

Her adrenaline was working overtime as she hurried through the stands to the stalls to get ready for her event. "Hey, Santos. Looks like you've got my Sassy all ready."

"Yep. She's perkier than usual tonight. You can't tell me horses aren't like people. She's excited to get out there and show her stuff."

Santos spoke Nikki's language. "Is that true?" She

rubbed Sassy's forelock. "You want to get out there and show off? Well, so do I. Let's do it."

After thanking Santos, she mounted her horse and walked her back past her competition. Now that Toly and Mills had accomplished another winning performance, Nikki could concentrate on what she had to do tonight.

She patted Sassy's neck. "You do seem a little friskier than usual. We had a good practice session earlier today and you know what's ahead." The wait seemed like forever before it was her turn to take off. "Here we go, Sassy."

From the moment they started down the alley, they seemed to go like the wind. Sassy circled both barrels with finesse. Now for the final one. But Nikki could tell her horse was going too fast. When she tried to square up around the third barrel, Sassy's right leg slid in reaction and sent them both banging into it.

Nikki was thrown to the ground and felt pain shoot up through her right leg when she tried to get to her feet. Nausea took over. She fell back and lay there for a few minutes while she waited for the ringing in her ears to stop. Voices were talking all around her. Someone started to examine her.

"Lie still, Ms. Dobson."

"But my horse— How's Sassy?"

"She's fine and being taken care of."

The Justin Sports Medicine Team had been the official health care provider for the PRCA for years. Nikki had seen them run to assist everyone who was hurt during an event, but she'd never dreamed she'd be the one who needed help.

Hot tears trickled out of her eyes. "I can't believe this has happened." One fatal slip and all her dreams had gone up in smoke.

"You're going to be fine too. Just let us do the work. We're going to stabilize you and get you to the hospital." By now they were taking her vital signs, but her head was still spinning.

"Nikki—" That was Mills's voice. Where was Toly? "I'm here. You're not alone."

Within seconds she was being transported out of the arena to a waiting ambulance. Once they'd helped her inside, she saw that her brother had come in and sat down beside her. He held her cowboy hat in his hand. His eyes were filled with tears while the attendants hooked up an IV and checked her vital signs again.

"Don't feel bad for me, Mills. It's life and we all take the risk when we get in the arena."

He shook his head. "This should never have happened to you."

"Sassy lost her footing. She was in extra high spirits after my workout with her today. I could feel it, but it doesn't matter now. How are you?"

"Don't worry about me."

"But I do, and you know it. Surely you realize Toly never wanted to hurt you."

"Let's not talk about that right now."

"All right. Do you have any idea how proud I am that you and Toly got a first-place win tonight? You'll never know how happy I am about that. Where is Toly?"

"He's gone to the South Point to pick up our buckles. He'll come to the hospital once the ceremony is over. We're both devastated for you. How's the pain?"

"We've given her something," the medic murmured.

"I'm floating right now."

"That's good."

"My car—"

"I'll take care of it later. You relax."

Her eyes closed. "Okay."

She had no sense of time. When they arrived at the hospital she was taken into the ER and sent up for a CT scan. When next she opened her eyes, it was after eleven. Mills stood against the curtain on the other side of the bed.

"Ms. Dobson? I'm Dr. Hall, the orthopedic surgeon on duty tonight. Your scan tells me you have a fractured fibula below the knee, but you won't require surgery."

"I'm thankful for that."

"I've told your brother that I'm going to put a cast on you and you'll have to wear it for six weeks. Barring any unforeseen circumstances, it should heal without problems and your leg will be as good as new. Knowing what a famous barrel racer you are, I suspect you'll be back on your horse competing again in no time."

No. There'd be no more competitions.

"Thank you, Doctor."

"The hospital is buzzing that there's a celebrity on-site from the Mack Center." He smiled. "A beautiful one, I might add."

"Your bedside manner is delightful."

He chuckled. "Okay. Let's get this done and we'll put you in a private room tonight."

Nikki was surprised how fast he applied the cast. "It's a blessing to be given such amazing care."

"It's been a pleasure. A nurse will come in and the orderlies will be here shortly to wheel you upstairs. I'll be by in the morning to check on you. We'll talk then about how to handle your crutches and what to expect after you go home."

"Thank you so much," she whispered.

She heard Mills chat with him for a minute before the doctor left the cubicle. Then he walked over to her side. "I'm thankful you didn't have to undergo surgery."

"Me too."

"The crew has texted me several times wanting to know how you are. They've promised to take expert care of your horses."

"I already know they will."

"Toly texted me too. He's on his way back from the hotel. I told him to check with the front desk about which room you're going to be put in."

"Good. I need to congratulate him on your win tonight." Her heart pounded extra hard. Even if she knew she looked terrible, she was living for the moment when she saw him again.

The nurse swept in. "Ms. Dobson? You've already been on the ten o'clock news."

"You mean my spectacular fall."

"Accidents happen, even to the most famous barrel racer in Las Vegas. Are you ready to be taken to your room?"

"Yes."

"You'll be moved shortly."

Mills leaned over to kiss her forehead. "I'll bring the bags with your clothes."

"What about my phone?"

"I've got it in my pocket."

"What would I do without you? I love you, Mills."

"Ditto. When I saw Sassy's leg slide like that, I almost went into cardiac arrest."

"I could tell she was taking that last turn too fast. Sassy was overly excited tonight."

"That's because she loves you and wanted to make you proud."

"I thought you didn't believe she had human feelings."

"Tonight's accident has made a believer out of me."

"Then let me make a believer out of you where Toly is concerned. Remember that he was afraid to let you down by telling you about his neuropathy, especially after what happened with Denise. Through thick and thin he's been your truest loyal friend every step of the way. In your heart you have to know that."

As they were talking, the curtain was swept back. The orderlies had come to transport her on the gurney. She gripped the handrails during the journey. It felt strange to be moving while she was still feeling the effects of the painkillers. Nikki didn't like it and hoped she wouldn't have to take any more.

They got out on the third floor. Mills walked at her side while they wheeled her down the hall past the nursing station to room 314. No sooner had she been put in the hospital bed than a new nurse walked in the room carrying a vase of glorious white and yellow daisies. The colors were so different from the red Christmas poinsettias she'd seen everywhere at this time of year that they came as a lovely surprise.

"Flowers already? How beautiful!"

"You must have an admirer, Ms. Dobson." She put it on the side table. "I'm Lynette. How are you feeling?"

"I'm not feeling much of anything."

"That means your medication is working." She checked Nikki's vital signs and made notations on the computer. "I'll be back."

Mills had been putting her clothes in the closet. She looked over at him. "Is there a card with those flowers? Are they from Toly?"

"I'll check." He walked over and pulled a little envelope off the pick. "Here you go."

"Do you mind reading it to me?"

"Sure." He pulled out the card. "Dear Nikki, may these flowers put spring back in your heart. Love, a friend."

Mills's mouth tightened. "I don't know why Toly didn't sign his name."

"It's not from him."

"How do you know?"

"He would have written a *T* on the card." She was positive they were from Denise. It was something her friend would have written. Nikki had an idea she was there at the hospital, waiting until she could visit her alone. But Nikki didn't want her brother to know the woman who'd broken his heart was nearby. Not yet.

A little white lie wouldn't come amiss. "I'm pretty sure they're from Jules McGinnis at the WPRA. That was very kind of her to send them."

When the door opened again, she held her breath because she hoped it would be Toly. But it was the nurse again, compounding her disappointment. This time she was holding a straw cowboy hat with a small floral arrangement nestled on the crown.

"You're a very popular person, Ms. Dobson."

She placed it right in her lap. Nikki handed Mills the card to read.

"Love, Laurie Rippon and all the gals."

Nikki bit her lip. "She's going to win the championship now. It was very kind of her to do this. It shows she's a champion inside and out."

She looked down and saw the names of all the finalists written around the brim with the words "National Finals Rodeo." One of the girls must have brought it to the hospital, maybe Laurie herself.

Nikki broke down in tears. Mills picked it up and studied the signatures. "There's a reason you were chosen as Miss Congeniality a year ago when you won the Miss Rodeo Montana Pageant." His voice sounded husky with emotion.

Just then the nurse came in one more time with a vase of pink roses and baby's breath. A ribbon that said WPRA was fastened to it.

Mills showed it to her before putting it on a side table. "I'm still wondering who your *friend* is since it wasn't from Jules McGinnis." He put the hat on the other stand in the room. "A secret admirer maybe?"

"I have no idea." She smiled at him. "Mills? Could you find the nurse and ask her if I can have a soda or something?"

"Sure. Be right back."

TOLY LEFT THE South Point at a quarter to eleven and hurried back to his rig to gather a few things before he took off for the hospital. En route he talked with his family, all of whom were thrilled for him, yet horrified for Nikki. Several of his close friends texted their congratulations.

At ten to midnight, Toly left the Flower Festival shop on the Strip. He carried a vase of Spanish Dream—large, brilliant red roses—protected with floral paper, and got in the car. He'd already called the hospital and couldn't get there fast enough. The operator told him Nikki had been taken to room 314.

Without wasting any time, he pulled into visitor parking and hurried inside to the main elevators. At the third-floor nursing station he checked to make sure he could visit Nikki. "We were both competing in the rodeo tonight. I couldn't get here any sooner."

One of the nurses said, "She's asleep, but you can peek in and deliver your flowers."

"Thanks. Is her brother here?"

"Yes. But he's down at the cafeteria getting a bite to eat."

Glad he'd be able to see her alone, Toly walked down the hall and opened the door to the dimly lit room. His beautiful Nikki lay on her back with the IV still attached to her hand. Her flowing black hair was splayed across the pillow. Hard to believe her right leg, now elevated, was encased in a cast from the knee down. A light sheet covered part of her gorgeous body.

He'd often thought she could play the role of Sleeping Beauty, but never more so than right now. Unfortunately, he didn't dare kiss her awake. She needed her sleep after the horrendous shock dealt to her.

With as much care as possible he put the flowers on the hospital tray table placed against the wall. He removed the paper around the roses. Their strong scent would fill the room before long. When she awakened, they were the first thing he wanted her to see.

Toly put his cowboy hat on a chair and sat down in the leather one. This was the first moment he'd had to relax since leaving his rig before the rodeo. Her fall had shaken him to the foundations. He extended his long legs, crossed them at the ankles and rested his head.

Nikki hadn't stirred. He began to think she'd stay asleep unless the nurse came in during the night to check her vital signs and woke her up. Just as he was reliving the scene in his head when he saw her horse slide into the barrel, he heard her voice.

"Mills?"

He got out of the chair and walked over to the side of the bed. "No. It's me."

"Toly—" Her voice throbbed. "I've been hoping you'd come."

"Did you honestly think I wouldn't?" He lowered his mouth to give hers a warm kiss. "What I want to know is, if this had to happen, why did it have to happen to you?"

"I thought the same thing when you told me about your neuropathy. But nothing has held you back. You're still on top."

"The only thing that matters to me is that you're all right so I can tell you how much I love you. Do you hear me?"

Chapter Eleven

Nikki's body started to tremble. "You...love me?"

"How could you possibly doubt it?"

She shook her head. "I don't. I don't. Oh, Toly—I love you, too. You just don't know how much. It seems like I've been waiting to hear you say that to me forever."

He kissed her again. "You know why I haven't, but I can't worry over how Mills feels about it any longer. I've been in love with you for an entire year."

"We've both been in pain. So many times I've been on the verge of blurting my love for you."

He covered her face with kisses. "Tonight I came close to death watching you slam into the barrel. Nikki—if I'd lost you, I couldn't have gone on living."

"You'll never lose me. It could never happen. You know I adore you. There isn't anything I wouldn't do for you. I love you heart and soul, Toly Clayton."

"Enough to marry me?"

She looked into his eyes. "Say that again."

"Will you marry me? Be my wife? Be the mother of our children one day?"

"Yes, my love!" she cried, trying to sit up, but he gently pushed her back.

"Even if I have this condition that might not clear up with surgery?"

"Surely you don't have to ask me that. Whatever you have to face, we'll do it together. I can't imagine a future without you, Toly. Ever since the rodeo started, I've been dreading the day it was over. I'm so used to being with you all the time, I want it to go on forever. I need you desperately."

"I've longed to hear those words from you." He reached in his pocket and pulled out a ring. "I had this made up for you months ago even though we haven't dated officially. I'm glad your IV is in your right hand, because this belongs on your left. I'm sorry I couldn't have asked your father for his blessing so I could marry you." He felt for her hand and slid it on her ring finger.

"Will you turn on the light so I can see?"

Toly rushed to do her bidding. She looked at the pear-shaped gray gemstone mounted in white gold. Her breath caught. "I've never seen anything so exquisite in my life."

"I have. But a person has to be able to look into your eyes. They're this exact color and pure as enchanted pools."

"Darling—" Her voice shook. "Where did you ever find a stone like this?"

"You once referred to me as the Sapphire Cowboy. There's a reason for that. My family owns a sapphire mine in the Sapphire Mountains on our ranch.

My mother has run the Clayton Sapphire Shop for a long time."

"Your mom is a jeweler?"

"At first it was a hobby, but she turned it into a real business. People came from all over to buy her sapphires."

"How fascinating!"

"We boys thought so too. One area called Gem Mountain produced over 180 million carats of sapphires for over 120 years. Before WWII people dug for the large stones, and the fragments were used for watch bearings in Switzerland. Later the rock hounds came to sift through them.

"Ages ago I looked in some of her velvet pouches and found the stone you're wearing. It's large, four carats, and exactly the color of your eyes. I had her mount it in white gold because I fell in love with your eyes along with everything else about you. The sapphires come in many colors. When you meet my three sisters-in-law, you'll see they each wear a sapphire engagement ring that matches their eyes."

"I can't wait to look at them and get acquainted with your whole family!"

"They're all going to love you."

"Is this really happening to me, or am I dreaming because of the medication?"

"I don't know. I've been taking painkillers too, but it all seemed real to me when I kissed you just now. What do *you* think?"

"I think I'm so in love, I'm delirious," she said as her brother came in the door.

"Whoops. I guess I'm interrupting something."

"No—" she called to Mills. "Toly and I have something important to tell you. Come on in."

His eyes took in the roses on the hospital tray table. "I guess you do. I take it the latest vase of roses is from you, Toly."

She blinked. "What roses?"

"These." Her brother picked up the vase and brought it over to the bed so Nikki could see them.

A gasp escaped her lips. "Oh, Toly—how gorgeous!"

"These Spanish roses are the same color as the embroidery on that black jacket you wore to dinner with me last week. You were stunning."

That was a magical night. She tore her eyes from Toly to look at her brother. "Tonight he asked me to marry him. Look at the engagement ring he gave me. It's a gray sapphire from his mother's sapphire shop on the ranch."

Mills looked closer. "Wow. Broken legs and engagement rings all in one night have left me spinning."

"Me too. Can I have a hug?"

Her brother went around the other side of the bed and gave her one. She could tell Mills was having a rough time taking it all in. "So, who are the daisies from?" he whispered.

She sucked in her breath. "I have no idea," she lied, "but right now I'm too happy to worry about anything. Thank you for being here for me, Mills. I love you."

"I love you too. If this makes you happy, then I'm happy for you."

"Goodness!" sounded an unfamiliar voice. The nurse

had just walked in. "It's the middle of the night. You gentlemen will have to leave."

Toly leaned over to give her one more kiss. "Get some sleep. We'll see you tomorrow after we get in some practice. Then we can stay with you until we have to drive over to the center. How does that sound, sweetheart?"

Sweetheart. He'd never called her that before. "I can't wait to see you."

"Good night." Mills kissed her cheek. She watched them leave the room, still incredulous that she wasn't dreaming.

"Well," the nurse said after checking her vital signs. "What's been going on here?"

"The man I love proposed to me tonight. He gave me this sapphire ring."

The nurse took hold of her hand. "How absolutely beautiful. You're a lucky woman to be engaged to that gorgeous blond hunk. Some women have all the luck. Kind of makes you forget your broken leg, right?"

Yes. She'd forgotten everything the moment Toly had told her he loved her and wanted to marry her.

"Get your sleep now."

"I will. Thank you."

"Nikki?"

Wednesday morning she looked up from the bed. "Denise—I'm so thrilled you're here. The doctor just left and they took out my IV. Now we've got time to talk before the guys come to the hospital."

Denise ran over and hugged her. "Let me see your ring."

She held out her hand and her friend squealed. "Toly was right. It matches your eyes. When I saw your accident, I never dreamed I'd see you looking this happy, Mrs. Clayton-to-be."

"*Mrs. Clayton.* To be his wife is the greatest wish of my life. I'm so happy, it's hard to contain. Forgive me for talking about myself. Thanks again for the beautiful daisies, Denise. Yours were the first flowers I received."

"I'm glad you liked them." She wandered over to the pink roses. "Who sent these?"

"Mills. They were delivered early this morning."

Her eyes grew misty. "How lovely." She kept moving. "There's no question who the red roses are from."

"No."

Denise picked up the straw cowboy hat. "What a wonderful gift to remember being in the rodeo. You'll treasure this forever."

"I know I will."

Finally, Denise pulled up a chair next to her and sat down. "Will you be released later to go back to the hotel? I'll drive you."

"Thanks for the offer, but no. The doctor is keeping me in the hospital until tomorrow so the therapist can work with me and my new crutches. It's probably for the best. Mills will be spared a night of fussing about me since the guys have another event tonight. I'm glad they won't be worrying about me.

"Besides, I'm such a klutz. The doctor joked that they put a cast on their patients and then send them home where a lot more damage is done by falling because they can't manage their crutches."

Her friend laughed and nodded. "That would be me for sure."

Nikki heard the sadness in her voice. "Denise? I've given everything a lot of thought and I think you should let Mills know you're here. He's so unhappy it breaks my heart."

"I'm afraid it will upset him too much."

"I disagree. So much has happened in the last twelve hours, I think to see you again would be the kind of relief he needs. Toly and I have each other. Now that he's asked me to marry him, I'm sure Mills is feeling more isolated than ever, emotionally."

"You don't know how worried I am about making everything worse."

"But how much worse can it be since you're not together now? Why not stay right here with me? I'll be getting a call from them soon. When I know the time they're coming, you can go down to the cafeteria. As soon as Mills walks in, I'll tell him you've come and are waiting for him. He can make up his own mind if he wants to talk to you or not. But nothing's going to happen if you don't make the first move."

"You're right. I'll think about it."

But not two minutes after she'd said those words, they heard a tap on the door. "Nikki?"

Her brother's voice. He hadn't phoned. "You're here!"

"Yep." He walked in her room without Toly.

Denise jumped up from the chair, white-faced. "Mills—"

The look on his face was a study in pure shock. "I

don't believe it." But Nikki saw no anger, for which she was grateful. By now he had to realize the daisies were from Denise.

"I—I've been in Las Vegas since the eighth so I could watch your events." Her voice faltered. "I told Nikki I came so I could talk to you. At first I thought it would be better if I waited until Finals were over. But we've been talking and I decided to be here when you came in. Would you be willing to come to my hotel? I'm staying at the Mirage. We can talk there in private."

Mills's face was masklike. "Why would I do that?"

"Because it's a matter of life and death."

Whoa. *Did you hear that, brother dear?*

The love in her fabulous brown eyes would melt any man on the spot. But not Mills. Maybe too much damage had been done. When he didn't say anything, Denise suddenly rushed out of the room.

Nikki girded up her courage. "Are you honestly going to let her go before you find out what she wanted? It took guts for her to come to Las Vegas, let alone face you."

He stood there with his hands on his hips. "What has she told you?"

"Everything." There was no point in lying.

"What is it about you?" he almost hissed the question.

"I don't understand what you mean."

"My own partner went to you about his neuropathy, not to me. The woman I wanted to marry broke it off, and now she shows up here to talk to you about it."

"Don't play dumb with me, Mills. With the national

championship at stake, if you'd been the one diagnosed with that condition, you would have done everything in your power to hide it from Toly in order not to let him down. As for Denise, she's in love with you. Always has been."

"How can you say that?"

"If you'll give her time to explain, you'll get answers to all your questions. Before you throw away your chance for a lifetime of happiness, just remember one thing. You never told her you were in love with her, that you wanted a future with her. A man can assume all he wants, but a woman needs to hear those words."

She paused, then said, "I was around Toly for a whole year, but I had to wait until tonight, after getting a broken leg no less, to hear them from Toly's lips for the first time."

His dark brows met in a frown. "Come on, Nikki. It was written all over him from the beginning."

"Really? I was hard-pressed to believe that after you warned me a year ago against Toly who was *the* ladies' man on the circuit and left broken hearts all over the country. For months I feared he was trying to charm me like he did the other cowgirls in his life. Amanda Fleming was a case in point."

She watched him swallow hard. Good. Maybe she was getting to him. "Have you seen Toly this morning?"

"I drove him to the center so he could pick up your rental car and use it. He's doing a few practice throws on the dummy before he comes. How soon are you being released? I'm here to take you back to the hotel."

"I can't go until tomorrow."

"Why? Is something wrong?"

"No. I have an appointment with the therapist to show me how to use crutches. The doctor will release me tomorrow morning. I'll have to watch tonight's event on TV. Do you want to stay and have lunch with me? I can ask them to bring you a tray."

"Do you want company?"

Well, well, well. That question was a dead giveaway. If Denise hadn't been the first sight he saw when he walked in, he would have sat down with Nikki and started a game of cards with her that would have lasted for hours.

"To be honest, I want to sleep. I didn't get enough last night. But thank you for offering to stay with me."

"If you're sure."

She yawned. "I'm positive."

"Then I'll be back later."

Want to bet? "Love you."

The second he left the room, she reached for her phone and called Toly. It was pure heaven to have the right. He picked up on the second ring. "Sweetheart?"

Heart attack. "How are you?"

"I woke up to a day like no other. I'm coming to get my fiancée and make you comfortable in my rig for the duration."

She couldn't stop smiling. "Mills was just here and offered to drive me to the hotel, but I can't leave until tomorrow. The therapist is going to help me learn how to walk with crutches."

A moan of protest escaped. "I'm so disappointed, but it's probably the best idea."

"I'm sure it is, but I'd rather be with you and never let you out of my sight."

"Amen. I love you, Nikki. I still can't believe you're going to marry me. We have a lot of plans to make."

"I know. I can't wait."

"How do you think Mills is taking the news?"

"I haven't had a chance to find out yet."

"Why?"

"When he walked in this morning, Denise was here."

"Dare I ask how that went?"

"She asked him to go to her hotel so they could talk." In the next breath, she told Toly about Mills's reaction. "He left just now instead of staying with me. We both know where he has gone. It's anyone's guess what will happen."

"Thank heaven she's come at last. He's been needing this in the worst way."

"I know. Denise was afraid it would throw him off his stride, but she loves him and knew it was time to tell him the truth."

"I guess we'll find out how things went if he shows up at the center tonight."

"He'll be there. But in what condition we can only guess."

"I'm putting my money on Denise getting through to him."

"So am I!" she cried. "How long will it take you to get here?"

"Ten minutes."

"Hurry."

"Sweetheart, before we hang up I need to talk to you about something."

Nikki's heart was listening. "What is it?"

"I don't know what's going to happen in the arena from here on out."

"No one knows, Toly. My accident taught me it's all a risk."

"Your spirit has taught me you're a champion's champion. But if it looks like Mills and I won't come out on top, it's him I'm worried about. I've never told you, but I've learned to love him like a brother."

With that admission, Nikki broke down sobbing quietly.

"Sweetheart?"

She cleared her throat. "He loves you too. I once told you that he worshipped you as a mentor. But over this last year I've seen that you've become like a brother to him and he hasn't wanted to share you with me. It's very sweet, really."

"Nikki…thank you for telling me that. I'll be there soon. We'll get my mother on the phone and give her our news. I'm her baby boy, the one she has worried about the most. I have a feeling our engagement isn't going to come as a surprise, not when I've spent every moment I could to be near you. She'll be overjoyed."

That was the word all right.

"See you in a minute."

TOLY LEFT THE hospital early after eating dinner with Nikki. Their call to his mother couldn't have come at a better time for his fiancée who needed the love of her parents. His mother welcomed her to the Clayton family with tears in her voice. Nikki's reaction had him leaving for the center walking on air.

Andy had saddled and bridled Snapper for him. "Have you seen Mills?"

"Not yet. Santos has Dusty ready for him."

He nodded. "I'm going to take Snapper for a walk. When Mills gets here, tell him I'll meet him near the boxes."

"Sure. How's Nikki? Her horses are missing her."

"Don't we know it. She's coming along just great. Do you want to hear a piece of news before anyone else tells you?"

"Of course."

"I asked Nikki to marry me. You and Santos will be invited to the wedding."

"Hallelujah! You're one lucky dude." Andy threw his arms around him, giving him a bear hug. Pain shot through Toly's upper right arm and shoulder, reminding him of his mortal weakness. Fortunately, he would be roping with his left arm tonight.

Toly pulled out a Pony Pop to feed Snapper. The memory of Nikki tossing him one that time in the barn came to mind. So much had happened in the last week, he was reeling.

When his horse had chomped it down, he mounted him and started walking him through the various contestants getting ready for their events. He was proud and thrilled to have made it this far, but whatever results transpired in the next few nights, he had the prize he wanted above all else. Nikki would be his forever. Beside her, any award or honor faded into insignificance.

The finalists for the team roping were starting to gather. In a minute he saw his partner ride toward him, filling him with relief. "Here we go again."

Toly couldn't tell from his demeanor how it had gone with Denise. "I'll try to do my best, Mills."

"Don't you think I know that?" Right now there was no way to say things right. They got in line. "I guess you told the crew you're getting married."

"Andy wanted to know how Nikki was getting along and it just came out. We called my mother and told her before I left the hospital. But I've made a big mistake I'd like to apologize for."

"What's that?"

"I should have asked your permission before I proposed to her."

"That's bull. I'm not her father."

"No. But you are her beloved brother. Last night when I saw her lying in that hospital bed with her leg in the cast, I lost it and everything came out."

The line started to move. Their turn was coming up fast.

"I have no right to complain when that proposal turned her life around last night."

His heart was heavy. "*Mills—*"

"We're up!"

Their names had been announced over the loudspeaker. Again Toly faced the box, this time with Nikki's declared love buoying him up. But his body could only do so much. For Mills's sake, he prayed there was another win in him. He glanced at his partner, then called for the steer.

No matter how many times he chased it, the experience was never the same. Tonight he used a Spanish flash loop and pulled a half head, which meant one horn and the nose. It was still legal, but not pretty. Good old Mills tied up the hind legs with expertise and they rode out of there.

The score to beat was 4.3. Toly matched it, but it was far from perfection. Mills came in at 4.4. The crowd went wild because they'd maintained their average. Somebody upstairs was still listening.

He rode back to the stalls. Mills wasn't far behind. But after he'd dismounted, he saw that his partner had disappeared, cheating him out of the chance to praise him.

Nikki had already texted him her congratulations and her love. After he got in her car, he phoned to tell her he was on his way to the hospital.

"Toly? More than anything in the world, I want you to come. But Mills just phoned me and said he has to talk to me alone."

He smothered a moan. "I understand. He's been in turmoil."

"I don't know how long he'll stay after he gets here, but—"

"Sweetheart, don't worry about it. He obviously needs you now. I'm going to head back to the rig. Call me after he leaves, no matter how late it is."

"I promise. You were spectacular out there."

"Thanks, but 4.3 won't win a championship."

"It did for tonight. Keep the faith."

"I love you, Nikki."

Toly stayed up, talking to his brothers, but by one o'clock her call hadn't come. Whatever was going on was serious. He flopped on the couch and waited before falling into oblivion.

NIKKI STARED AT her brother who'd just walked into her hospital room. "Mills—what are you doing here this late?" She'd hoped he would be with Denise right now.

"I need to talk to you and hoped you wouldn't be asleep."

"I'm wide-awake. Come and sit by me."

He drew a chair up to the side of the bed. "I've been talking to Denise and told her I don't want to see her anymore. She won't be coming to the hospital."

A groan came out of Nikki.

"She told me about Johnny Rayburn coming back from war without a hand. It put a horrifying picture in my head. I could understand her compassion for him. But I don't get why she couldn't have talked it over with me instead of just breaking up with me."

"Do you remember the conversation you and I had earlier?"

"What do you mean?"

"About Toly who didn't propose until last night? Until he said the words, I didn't know how he truly felt. You thought of course it was obvious, but I'll say it again. I knew he was interested, but it wasn't obvious to me that he wanted to make a lifetime commitment to me and marry me. There's a difference between being someone's girlfriend and being *the* woman for all time."

"But—"

"No buts, Mills. Denise reacted exactly the way I would have acted. She needed to know you wanted her to be your wife. Without that reassurance she had to deal with Johnny the best way she could. His PTSD was a huge factor. She believed she was doing the right thing to give you your freedom while she helped let Johnny down gently. How did she know what your plans would be once the rodeo was over? What if you met another woman in the meantime?"

"That's crazy!"

"To you, because you knew you loved her. But not to her. She came to Las Vegas because she loves you and wanted to support you. It took a lot of courage. If you want to know the truth, I admire her for letting you go instead of clinging to you when you didn't make your intentions clear. There's nothing more pathetic than a woman or a man who hangs on hoping and hoping for something that might never happen.

"She's the real deal, Mills, and beautiful inside and out. Of course it's your decision. Now if you don't mind, I love you dearly, but that last medication has made me so sleepy I can't keep my eyes open."

"Sorry I've kept you up this late." He got out of the chair and kissed her cheek.

"Don't ever be sorry. See you tomorrow."

Chapter Twelve

When Thursday morning came, Toly was surprised to discover he'd slept on the couch all night. The call from Nikki had never come. He got up and wandered in the kitchen to get himself a cup of coffee before he phoned her.

His laptop was open and he discovered he'd received a message from his neurologist. Toly opened it.

Dear Mr. Clayton—

I told you I would get back to you when I'd done more research on your condition. The doctors in Paris just let me know that they don't feel ready to perform surgery on you before summer. Probably July.

In the meantime, I'm corresponding with another team of doctors at the Mayo Clinic. Again their timetable is probably June at the earliest. I've sent both groups your medical history and they'll contact me with further information as we get closer to those dates.

If you've had another episode since visiting my office, I'd like you to call me as soon as you can.

I'll ask my receptionist to put you through immediately.

Dr. Moore.

The doctor had left his phone number.

Toly frowned, deciding to make the call now. Within
two minutes they were connected.

"Mr. Clayton—"

"Hello, Dr. Moore. You said to call if I'd had another
episode, which I did a couple of nights ago during the
competition. Is that alarming?"

"In the same hand?"

"Yes."

"Nowhere else?"

"No."

"It's not alarming, but it shows your rope throwing is aggravating your condition and the surgery can't
come too soon."

"I realize that, but I want to know why you keep asking me if I have symptoms somewhere else."

"I don't think you're going to, but some patients de-
velop problems in their feet too. You have a unique case.
All the readouts on you lead me to believe that with the
surgery, you shouldn't have more problems."

He gripped the phone tighter. "If I do, just tell me
one thing. Is my disease fatal?"

"No, Mr. Clayton. People with this condition live out
their life span like anyone else. It's not life threatening.
The last thing I want is for you to sink into a depression over it or let it affect your ranching or personal
life in any way."

Toly was reading between the lines. "You're talking about women."

"Yes. You can expect to live a fulfilled life with a wife and children. You're in your twenties and in excellent physical health and shape. With the exercise you get, you're doing all the right things. Any future progression of this condition, if there is any, is still too many years away to even think about.

"I've been following your rodeo competition and have learned that you and your partner are still in the lead to win the overall championship. I have every confidence that you'll maintain it to the end. You have a warrior's spirit. The best of luck to you and stay in touch."

After they hung up Toly realized the earliest he could do anything about his condition would be summer. But right now he had Nikki on his mind. After a quick shower, he needed to get over to the hospital. She'd be going home today. He couldn't wait!

NIKKI GRIPPED HER cell phone tighter. "Denise? What did you say?" She could hardly hear her friend for the tears.

"Mills came to the hotel last evening. I can't get into it, but he asked me not to visit or call you. I'm going back to Great Falls today."

Her words brought pain to Nikki, who'd hoped they had worked things out. "I really thought he could forgive you. Under the circumstances, I'll call you after I know you're home. I love you, Denise."

"I love you too."

Just then Toly's tall, rock-hard body walked into her hospital room. Never did she need him more.

"Sweetheart," he cried softly when he saw her wet cheeks and put out his left arm to hug her. "What's happened?"

Nikki buried her face against his chest. "Mills went to see Denise yesterday and it didn't go well. She's leaving on the next plane and has been told not to call or visit me."

Toly ran his hands through her hair. "I can't say I'm surprised. Mills has made himself scarce."

"I can't believe it."

"What can't you believe?"

Another voice had sounded. It was her orthopedic surgeon. She hadn't realized he'd walked in. "Next year I expect to see you back in Las Vegas again to finish what you started."

"That's not why I'm crying." She gave a sad laugh and brushed the moisture off her face. "Doctor? This is my fiancé, Toly Clayton."

They shook hands before Toly sat down to give her doctor room to check her out. "I'm releasing you this morning. How did it go with the therapist?"

"I had no idea how hard it is to use crutches, but with practice I'm sure I'll get the hang of it."

"You will. I'm aware you'd like to go to the center to watch your brother and fiancé perform for the rest of the rodeo, but I would caution you to stay down in your hotel and keep your leg elevated until you fly home."

"But, Doctor—I can't stay away on the last night."

"You can watch everything on TV."

"But if they win the overall, I want to see them receive their award at the South Point Hotel afterward."

"Then I suggest you have a bodyguard to help protect you so you're not accidentally knocked down. I don't want to see you in here again." He said it with a smile, but she knew he meant it.

He turned to Toly. "I take it you're driving her to the hotel?" He nodded. "Then I'll ask the nurse to come in with the wheelchair and the instructions I'm sending with you. When you get back home, you'll want to contact an orthopedic surgeon there to do any follow-up and remove your cast."

"Thank you so much. You've all been wonderful."

"That's nice to hear. I'm sorry you couldn't finish your brilliant run for the barrel championship. I'm sure you would have won it." He turned to Toly. "Good luck to you. Everyone's betting on you and your partner."

"Thank you, Doctor. No one's more precious to me than Nikki. I'm very grateful to you."

After he walked out, Toly gave her a quick kiss on the lips. "I'm going to carry all your flowers down to the car, then I'll come back for you."

"Toly? Wait. The doctor had to warn me, but I plan to be out there for your performances."

He shook his head. "No you're not. He was right. There's so much pandemonium, it'll be more difficult with crutches. I'll need the peace of mind knowing you're at the hotel. By the way, I plan to spend the rest of my nights in your hotel room.

"Before we left for Las Vegas, I had this dream of being your roommate and luring you into loving me.

What I didn't envision was being your nurse, but I'll take it because I'm madly in love with you."

NIKKI FOUND OUT over the next few days that no man could have been a sweeter more tender lover who hadn't made love to her completely yet, let alone a better nurse. The first thing she'd noticed when he'd brought her to the hotel was her little Christmas tree lit up.

He was so wonderful and waited on her hand and foot. They played cards. He brought her the chocolate marshmallow ice cream she craved and virtually showered her with the kind of love she could never have imagined.

The downside of all this was Mill's absence, except to show up at the center in time for the team roping event both evenings. After two scores that put them in second place, they'd tied with Shay's team for first place in the overalls. Tonight one of the teams would pull ahead to be the grand champions.

Toly put on a tough front, but she knew deep in his heart how devastated he was for Mills and the crisis he was going through. There could be no joy when the two of them were both worried sick about him and Denise.

Too soon they finished eating dinner and she was propped on the couch with her leg extended. Toly was about to leave for the center one last time. She gripped his hands and looked up at him. "I want to be there. My heart is with you and Mills."

"I know that. It's why I can go out there tonight, whatever happens."

"Has your family arrived yet?"

"Yes."

"*Toly*—". She sat up to embrace him, kissing him with all the urgency of her soul.

"I'll be back."

The minute he walked out the door, she burst into tears. Nikki was an emotional mess. She quickly turned on the TV with the remote to watch the lead-up to the rodeo. Anything to keep her from going crazy.

It was so surreal to be there trapped in a cast instead of being at that arena to get ready for her event.

It was so awful to think her brother was in terrible turmoil because of a broken heart.

It was so unbelievable that Toly had a strange neuropathy that had forced him to throw with his left arm, never knowing what would happen.

It was torture not to be able to be there tonight for the man she adored.

It killed her that her parents weren't alive to lean on, that Toly's father wasn't alive to cheer him on.

Nikki's list of pain kept growing until the rodeo actually started. She sat back to watch the events. But her heart was thudding too fast when it came time for the team roping.

She'd never heard such noise coming from the arena and couldn't seem to calm down. There was a tie between Toly and Shay. But because Toly and Mills had come in to the events with the overall lead, they would ride last with Shay and his partner just ahead of them.

So far the time to beat tonight was 3.8. Shay tore out of the gate and they snagged the steer with a 3.6, 3.8.

Now it was Toly's turn. The crowd noise level went up. She didn't think she could watch.

Thump, thump. Thump, thump went the beat of her heart. The camera panned to Mills wearing his steely look. Then it settled on Toly in the box. There he was holding the rope in his right hand, the ultimate cowboy in every sense of the word. Though she knew his upper arm and shoulder still pained him a great deal, he was going for it.

Oh please, please. With everything that had gone wrong, make this one moment right. No episode tonight. The gray sapphire on her finger reminded Nikki she already had her prize. Now it was their turn.

Out came the steer. Almost immediately the horns had been caught and before she knew it, the hind legs were sweetly tied up. She heard the announcer.

"Toly Clayton and Mills Dobson have just swept this year's Wrangler Team Roping Championship in an epic 3.2, 3.4 win."

In her joy, Nikki jumped up from the couch, forgetting all about her leg and lost her balance. Thank heaven she fell backward. She laughed because the doctor had been right and she hadn't even been using her crutches.

She grabbed her phone to send a text.

Darling Toly. Words can't express. Just wait till you come back later.

Nikki sent another one to Mills.

Dearest brother. There's no one like you. Tonight I'm positive the folks in heaven are rejoicing with me.

Their year of hard, grueling work, of exhausting travel over thousands of miles on the circuit, was over. She couldn't comprehend it as she waited for the barrel racing.

For once it was pure pleasure to watch each finalist fly into the arena. They were fabulous. All of them. She thought about the hat they'd signed and would never forget. Just as she'd imagined, Laurie Rippon rode out last and won the championship with a 13.48. No one deserved it more. She sent her a text congratulating her.

With it was finally over, she got up with the aid of her crutches to get herself a cola from the minifridge. It would be several hours yet before Toly and Mills would be able to leave for the South Point. She had no idea of her brother's plans, but she couldn't worry about that right now. Nikki needed to throw her arms around Toly and never let him go.

To her surprise, she heard a knock on the door and knew it couldn't be Denise. Since she was already up, she hobbled to the door with her crutches and opened it.

"Mills—" He wasn't alone. "Denise—"

Nikki knew what this meant. In the next breath she grabbed them. They did a three-way hug, crutches included. She started to sob for happiness and couldn't stop. "Now all my dreams have come true."

"So have mine." Denise had broken down too. "Want to see what Mills gave me before tonight's event?" She put out her left hand where a diamond ring sparkled on her finger.

Nikki looked at her brother, who wore an ecstatic smile. "You told me Denise needed to know how I felt about her. I took your advice, but the truth is I've been carrying it around for months."

"Now he tells us!" Nikki cried. "I'm so happy for you two, I want to race around the arena and shout it to the world that my favorite people are in love and going to get married. Come all the way in and sit down. I want to hear everything.

"Does Toly know?" she asked after they got settled.

He shook his head.

"He's going to die when he finds out."

Mills had pulled Denise onto his lap. "We know he's coming to get you. We thought we'd surprise him when we show up at the South Point for the medal ceremony."

"This is the best news in the world. Here I was in despair because I could picture you at the airport taking off."

"She almost did. I had to race to get there in time."

Denise looked radiant. "I waited before leaving to hear the scores for him and Toly. While I was sitting in the lounge before we boarded, I heard Mills call out, "You can't leave, Denise! I've got something for you!"

"You're kidding—how romantic!"

"It was. He ran up to me and in front of everyone got down on one knee and proposed. I couldn't believe it until he slid this ring on my finger. All the people in the lounge clapped."

"Who wouldn't? I wish I had pictures. Let me take

some now with my phone." Nikki pulled it out of her pocket and snapped half a dozen in succession. "Come on. One big kiss for posterity. Toly will want to see it."

Her normally reserved brother reached around and gave his fiancée a kiss to die for. Nikki made a video of it while she hooted and hollered.

When he finally let her go, he turned to Nikki. "Thank you for making me see reason."

Tears rolled down Denise's cheeks. "Thank you for being the best friend a girl ever had."

"What a night for celebrating!"

Denise nodded. "Speaking of that, we need to get back to my hotel so I can change before we drive over to the South Point." She slid off his lap.

Mills walked over to hug Nikki. "We'll see you there in a little while."

"Most definitely."

Not two minutes after they left, she heard a loud rap on her hotel room door. That was odd. "Yes?" she called out. "Who is it?"

"Toly gave us a card key." *Us?* "Can we come in?"

"Yes," she said in a hesitant voice.

The door opened and in walked his three hunky brothers she'd only seen on his cell phone gallery. They wore his smile and all had inherited the Clayton charm and fabulous looks.

"I'm Wymon." The dark-haired one spoke first. "Our brother was right about his fiancée. You *are* gorgeous. By the way, this is Roce and that's Eli. According to Toly, the doctor said you would need a bodyguard if you wanted to see the ceremony in person. So the three of us have come to do the job. Our mom is already at the South Point with Toly and they're waiting for us."

"Oh my gosh." Thank goodness she'd done her makeup and had changed into her outfit so she'd be ready when he came.

"I'm glad you're ready because we don't want to miss anything."

Since Toly had loved the black outfit with the red embroidery, Nikki had chosen to wear it. She kept on the sandal she was wearing.

The one named Roce whistled. "You're on time too. Our bro is a lucky man."

"He says he belongs to the best family on earth and can't wait to help all of you on the ranch."

Eli, the dark-brown-haired brother, grinned at her. "That's when we're all going to get tired of hearing about the beautiful rodeo queen he was determined to rope for himself. But it looks like you roped him. Want me to carry your bag?"

She laughed. "Would you?"

"I'd be honored."

The next twenty minutes became a blur as they helped her out to a limo and escorted her to the South Point. As usual, the place was packed, but since it was the last night of Finals, there was an energy she'd never felt before.

They cleared the way for her to the front where she suddenly saw Toly sitting with his mother, their heads close together while they talked. Her heart did a thunderclap to see him decked out in his Western gear and Stetson.

Roce walked ahead and alerted Toly, who jumped up and turned around. Like in a dream, he moved toward her, his green eyes ablaze with joy and light. For tonight their win had changed him. She didn't see any sadness. He came close and swept her and her crutches into his arms—even if he was hurting—and kissed her in front of everyone.

"I love you, Toly. I love you."

Wymon patted his shoulder. "Come on, bro. We're all due on stage."

"Let's go, sweetheart."

"What do you mean?"

"You're coming with us."

Before she could think, the whole Clayton clan helped her go up onstage with him. But nothing could have shocked Toly more than to see Mills and Denise waiting for them. He had his arm around her and they both glowed.

Toly whispered, "If I'm having a hallucination, don't bring me out of it."

"It's no hallucination. Mills stopped her from leaving town. I'm sure he'll tell you the details later, but just before your brothers came to pick me up, Mills brought Denise to the hotel. They're getting married. Wouldn't it be exciting if we made it a double wedding?"

Mills walked over and hugged Toly hard. "Forgive me for everything."

"I will if you'll forgive me. After all, we're brothers."

"Yes, we are," Mills said with tears in his eyes.

Then Toly squeezed her waist. "Come on, sweetheart. We have to sit down so our award ceremony can begin. Then we're on our own."

AFTER SAYING GOODBYE to Mills, who was flying back to Great Falls with Denise on Sunday morning, Toly loaded Nikki into his rig with her bags. He planned to drive her home, driving straight through so they could be alone. The crew had the job of returning the rental cars and taking all four horses back in the Dobson rig.

Toly knew Nikki wondered why they weren't flying too. But he needed time to tell her something. He dreaded it. Depending on her reaction, there might not be a wedding, after all.

She insisted on sitting in front next to him while he drove. Fortunately she could bend her leg. They'd stopped to stock up on snacks and drinks. Hard to believe they'd never driven in one of their rigs together on their way to a rodeo on the circuit. They could have done when they'd both been featured at different venues. But Mills had set the boundaries.

Now there were no boundaries. But a new hard cruel fact had arisen that could change everything in an instant. As the sun went down, it started to snow. The time seemed right to tell her what was on his mind. If they ran into a blizzard, then he'd stop at a lay-by until it stopped.

She smiled at him. "This is so cozy. I've had dreams about living with you in this rig."

She didn't know the half of it. "Nikki?"

"What is it, darling?"

"I have something important to tell you before you go to bed."

"I'm not ready for that yet."

"But you need to rest your leg."

"Obviously you've got something important on your mind."

"I need you to think about something hard. After I've taken you home, I'll be driving to the ranch. I won't call you until you've had a few days to deal with it."

"Deal with what? You're scaring me."

"If it weren't scary, we wouldn't be having this discussion."

"I don't know you like this, Toly!"

"I'm sorry, sweetheart. I don't know how to do this any other way."

He could hear her struggling. "Go on."

"I need to tell you everything about my neuropathy." For the next fifteen minutes he laid it out for her, sparing her nothing. She had to understand what could happen to his legs and feet, arches and toes. In time he might even have difficulty breathing or swallowing.

"This condition can affect your sense of touch, how you feel pain and temperature. One of the symptoms is a weakening of muscle strength. Another symptom might be losing your balance. It could be hard to do things that require coordination. I might get to the point that it would affect my walking, let alone fastening buttons."

"Stop! I've heard enough. The only thing I know is that you have a problem in your right hand and lower arm."

"But it could get worse, "Toly murmured. She shook her head. "I'm not going to listen."

"Please hear me out. The doctor told me I'd live out the years given to me, but at what price? I don't want a wife who has to push me around in a wheelchair. Last night I realized I shouldn't have proposed to you, but I love you too much. You don't want to marry a man who is already becoming an invalid."

"That's ridiculous, Toly. I won't listen."

"I was wrong to give you that ring. You shouldn't have to be tied to a man in my condition."

"Are you asking me to give it back?"

"I made a mistake. Now I'm begging you to sleep on this for a few days while you allow the reality of what I've said to sink in."

He heard her sharp intake of breath. "I don't need a few days. I can't believe the great Toly Clayton, the cowboy who was crowned king of the headers last night is ready to throw in the towel today. Am I even talking to the same person?"

"Nikki—"

"I don't want to hear another word." She reached for her crutches and stood up. "I'm going to bed. In the morning I want you to stop at the nearest airport and I'll fly the rest of the way home. Considering that you could be falling apart anytime now, I'm surprised you wanted to drive me at all."

She tossed the ring at him and hobbled away faster than he could have imagined. Dear God. What had he done?

"Toly? Are you awake yet? Solana, the housekeeper, tried to get you to come down to breakfast, but she said you didn't answer."

He rolled over and sat up. "I was awake all night and barely got to sleep. I don't feel like talking right now."

"I'm not the person who wants to talk to you, but if that's the way you feel, then I'll send her away."

Could it possibly be Nikki? After what he'd said to turn her inside out, he never thought to see her again.

"Wait, Mom—" But she didn't answer back.

Like lightning he jumped out of bed, pulled on a pair of jeans and a T-shirt. Then raced out of the room and down the stairs to the living room. The traditional tall Christmas tree with its multicolored lights dominated the interior. Its glow illuminated his former fiancée standing in front of a wall of family pictures, using her crutches for support. She was a breathtaking sight in a Western Levi's skirt and cherry-red sweater.

"Nikki?"

She turned and eyed him with a laser-like glance that was discomfiting. "I've been looking at everyone, all ages and sizes. After reading online, I understand that your condition is inherited, but I don't see one of your relatives who's in a wheelchair."

"Listen, I—"

"No. You listen. As I recall you told me to go home and think about this for a few days while I dealt with it. The question is, have *you* dealt with it? You look perfectly healthy to me right now. I don't see you weaving or wobbling on your feet. You even had enough strength to close the fly on your jeans before you flew down here like you were coming out of the alley."

He shook his head. "I can't believe you just said that."

"I do have a brother, you know, and I couldn't believe all that drivel you told me in the rig." She handled her crutches with amazing dexterity and walked right up to him. "Where's my ring?"

"Upstairs."

"I'd like you to put it on me again."

Toly had never been so humbled in his life. "Sweetheart, I—"

"I think you ought to stop talking and go get it. That is, if you can, or have you lost feeling in your feet?"

"It isn't funny, Nikki."

"No, it isn't. So let's have all the fun we can before I have the joy of wheeling you around. You know— a wedding, a wedding *night*! A honeymoon? I called your doctor.

"After talking to him, maybe we can plan a late one after you're operated on in Paris. I'd much rather go there than the Mayo Clinic. You and I have lived an inbred life in our horsey world. It's time we found out why everyone says that if you haven't been to France, you haven't lived."

"Would you be willing to live in the rig until our ranch house is built?"

"I've been planning on it. Denise will be moving into the ranch house with Mills. I told you before, the rig felt like our home while we were in Las Vegas."

"I was never happier in my life than being there with you. Just so you know, Mom gave me a piece of land up the road. She and Dad talked about it before he died. It's the perfect spot to build our ranch house. But with the snow, it probably won't be ready until late spring."

"I don't care how long it takes."

"After Christmas we'll hire an architect."

"I was thinking the four of us could get married two weeks from today, if that's all right with your family. We'll do a reception here and another one in Great Falls."

He nodded. "I'll be right back."

Solving the problem of levitation for all time, he flew through the house and up the stairs to get her ring out of his dresser drawer. On the way down, he almost ran over his mother at the landing.

She cupped his face in her hands. "That woman is pure gold and more valuable than all the gold buckles you ever won." He'd finally told his mother about his neuropathy.

His eyes smarted. "I know." He hugged her hard before hurrying into the living room. Nikki stood near the tree, balancing on her crutches with her right arm while she extended her left hand.

He walked over and slid the ring home. "Thank heaven for you," he murmured against her lips and rocked her in his arms for a long, long time. The crutches fell to the floor, but they didn't care.

Chapter Thirteen

Nikki grabbed the playing cards and looked up at Toly from her side of the bed wearing only a sheet. Since their church wedding in Stevensville, they'd spent the last three days and nights in the rig decorated for Christmas by her new sisters-in-law. They'd put up a fabulous Christmas tree and had hung garlands that stretched from one end of the rig to the other.

Potted red poinsettias had been placed around his bedroom that had become their bedroom. The whole rig smelled of pine and Nikki was so in love, she never wanted to leave it or his arms.

"You're a cheater, Mr. Clayton, but I can't figure out how you do it."

"So you've noticed I have another skill besides cooking, Mrs. Clayton."

"You're fishing for compliments again. Are you ready for a post Christmas present?"

"You've showered me with too many."

"This one is different and my personal favorite. You'll have to get out of bed. It's up on the top shelf of the closet in the hallway."

"I didn't know that."

"I had a hard time trying to figure out where to keep it out of sight until now."

He kissed a certain spot. "I'll be right back."

Nikki watched her gorgeous husband pull on the bottom half of his sweats and leave the room for a minute. When he returned, he had to remove the Christmas wrapping from the fourteen-by-eighteen framed photograph.

She heard him suck in his breath. "*Nikki*— Where? How? When did you take this picture?"

"Last summer while you were out in the corral with Snapper practicing some throws, I was upstairs and saw you out the window. It was hot. You took off your shirt and had just dipped your Stetson in the rain barrel before putting it on your head. I thought you were the most amazing male specimen I'd ever seen in my life.

"Without hesitation I reached for my camera and took a dozen pictures of you. After having them developed, I decided I loved this one best. The art studio enlarged it to this size and I had it made up in black and white. The silver-and-black frame with the clear glass cover looks perfect with it. Did you see the plaque at the bottom?"

He looked down. In a husky voice he said, "The Sapphire Cowboy."

"Yup. One day our children will regard this as a great treasure to cherish forever. I know I do. If you'll notice, the white gold band on my ring finger makes the perfect frame for my gray sapphire, another treasure."

Toly rested the photograph against the wall. "Just a minute. I'll be right back."

What was he up to?

In a minute he came back and handed her a gift of approximately the same size. "It's your turn."

Excited, she undid the wrapping and there was one of her posters. The kind she'd given out at the dealership in Great Falls before they'd left for Las Vegas. It was in glorious color and framed in a light oak color.

"Oh, Toly—"

He smiled. "I grabbed one when you weren't looking and planned to hang it in the tack room on the ranch. But everything has changed since then and I wanted us to have it. There's a plaque at the bottom."

She couldn't believe it and looked down. My Sweet Clover Sweetheart.

Her eyes filled with tears. "I can't believe it."

He put both pictures against the far wall and got back in bed. "Consider this an after Merry Christmas gift, my love. Now why don't we call it a night."

"I thought you'd never suggest it," she teased.

"You little hussy." He turned off the lamp at the side of the bed and leaned over her. "I don't know how it's possible, but my hunger for you just keeps growing."

He started devouring her. They made love again. She never wanted it to stop. Each time he touched her, it thrilled her so much she moaned in ecstasy. Amazing how her cast didn't interfere with the pleasure they brought to each other.

In the middle of the night Nikki awoke, wishing he weren't asleep. She caressed the dusting of hair on his chest. He was such a beautiful man and almost too wonderful to be real. She'd known him for a year and couldn't believe she'd been lucky enough to have married him.

"I heard that sigh," he murmured, kissing her throat. "You're awake."

"Yes. It sounded serious."

"It was. I think I love you too much."

"Then we suffer from the same condition." He plunged his hands in her hair. "I've been worried you'd wake up before now and tell me you need a day away from me."

Nikki laughed and slid halfway on top of him. "I've been worried what your family will think. We haven't gone outside once."

"We're in the middle of a blizzard right now."

"Still—"

His deep chuckle permeated her body. "With three brothers who are crazy about their wives, you know exactly what they're thinking."

"It's kind of embarrassing."

"It's kind of wonderful to be this much in love, sweetheart. I still can't believe you wanted to marry me knowing what could be ahead of me."

"We're not going to talk about that. Neither of us knows what the future will hold. Do you remember when we both got excited about riding in the rodeo? We didn't think about the risk. It was too much fun doing something we were good at."

"I remember. I was obsessed."

"So was I. It didn't matter what we had to go through.

We loved it so much we kept going back for more. That's how I feel about our marriage. Every day, every night is a great adventure. I never want to miss a moment of it, darling."

"We're not going to."

"No we're not. So let's not use birth control. I want to get pregnant with your baby as soon as we can. I'm jealous of your sisters-in-law and can't wait to have an adorable little boy or girl like Libby."

"You mean it?"

"Oh, Toly. I can't wait to fill those bedrooms we're going to have designed for our new house. Wouldn't it be fantastic if we had children who love the rodeo too?"

"What if they don't?"

"It doesn't matter because you're going to make the most terrific father. You had a wonderful role model."

"He was the best." Toly kissed her with tenderness. "So were your parents."

"You never knew them."

"No. But I know you. You're my favorite person in the world. Mills comes in a close second."

"What a beautiful thing for you to say. I'm crazy about your family too." She kissed his mouth. "Love me again, Toly."

He began kissing her back with growing desire. "I thought you'd never ask."

* * * * *

COMING NEXT MONTH FROM

HARLEQUIN®

Western Romance

Available January 2, 2018

#1673 THE BULL RIDER'S VALENTINE

Mustang Valley • by Cathy McDavid

When Nate Truett and Ronnie Hartman are thrown together to help with the local rodeo, they are still healing from a tragic past. Yet an old attraction prevails. Will a Valentine's Day proposal bring them together for good?

#1674 COWBOY LULLABY

The Boones of Texas • by Sasha Summers

Years ago, cowboy Click Hale broke Tandy Boone's heart. Now he's her neighbor and a father to a beautiful daughter. How can Tandy start over with a reminder of everything she lost living right next door?

#1675 WRANGLING CUPID'S COWBOY

Saddle Ridge, Montana • by Amanda Renee

Rancher and single dad Garrett Slade can't stop thinking about Delta Grace, the beautiful farrier who works for him. He's finally ready to take the next step, but he senses she has a secret...

#1676 THE BULL RIDER'S TWIN TROUBLE

Spring Valley, Texas • by Ali Olson

Bull rider Brock McNeal loves to live on the edge. But when he starts to fall for Cassie Stanford, a widow with twin boys, Brock's in a whole different kind of danger!

YOU CAN FIND MORE INFORMATION ON UPCOMING HARLEQUIN® TITLES, FREE EXCERPTS AND MORE AT WWW.HARLEQUIN.COM.

HWESTCNM1217

Get 2 Free Books,
Plus 2 Free Gifts—
just for trying the
Reader Service!

HARLEQUIN®
Western Romance

THE BULL RIDER'S COWGIRL
APRIL ARRINGTON

HER COLORADO SHERIFF
PATRICIA THAYER

YES! Please send me 2 FREE Harlequin® Western Romance novels and my 2 FREE gifts (gifts are worth about $10 retail). After receiving them, if I don't wish to receive any more books, I can return the shipping statement marked "cancel." If I don't cancel, I will receive 4 brand-new novels every month and be billed just $4.99 per book in the U.S. or $5.74 per book in Canada. That's a savings of at least 12% off the cover price! It's quite a bargain! Shipping and handling is just 50¢ per book in the U.S. and 75¢ per book in Canada.* I understand that accepting the 2 free books and gifts places me under no obligation to buy anything. I can always return a shipment and cancel at any time. Even if I never buy another book, the two free books and gifts are mine to keep forever.

154/354 HDN GLPV

Name _____ (PLEASE PRINT) _____

Address _____ Apt. # _____

City _____ State/Prov. _____ Zip/Postal Code _____

Signature (if under 18, a parent or guardian must sign)

Mail to the **Reader Service:**
IN U.S.A.: P.O. Box 1867, Buffalo, NY 14240-1867
IN CANADA: P.O. Box 611, Fort Erie, Ontario L2A 9Z9

Want to try two free books from another line?
Call 1-800-873-8635 or visit www.ReaderService.com.

*Terms and prices subject to change without notice. Prices do not include applicable taxes. Sales tax applicable in N.Y. Canadian residents will be charged applicable taxes. Offer not valid in Quebec. This offer is limited to one order per household. Books received may not be as shown. Not valid for current subscribers to Harlequin Western Romance books. All orders subject to credit approval. Credit or debit balances in a customer's account(s) may be offset by any other outstanding balance owed by or to the customer. Please allow 4 to 6 weeks for delivery. Offer available while quantities last.

Your Privacy—The Reader Service is committed to protecting your privacy. Our Privacy Policy is available online at www.ReaderService.com or upon request from the Reader Service.

We make a portion of our mailing list available to reputable third parties that offer products we believe may interest you. If you prefer that we not exchange your name with third parties, or if you wish to clarify or modify your communication preferences, please visit us at www. ReaderService.com/consumerschoice or write to us at Reader Service Preference Service, P.O. Box 9062, Buffalo, NY 14240-9062. Include your complete name and address.

HWR17R

SPECIAL EXCERPT FROM

♥ HARLEQUIN®

Western Romance

Rodeo cowboy Brock McNeal doesn't date women with kids. So why can't he stop thinking about single-mom Cassie Stanford?

Read on for a sneak preview of
THE BULL RIDER'S TWIN TROUBLE,
the first book in Ali Olson's
SPRING VALLEY, TEXAS series!

Brock hurried up the steps to the front porch, noting the squeaking of the stairs and the flaking white paint.

He hoped the widow didn't expect him to be working there too often. If his mother was so desperate to have him around, why would she give him a big job that might eat into all the time he had at home?

Brock brushed the question aside and knocked. He'd go through a short introduction and make his way back for his hot meal, then he'd begin preparing for his next rodeo.

After a few seconds, the door opened and any thought of food or rodeos disappeared. He stared, caught off guard by the lovely woman who stood there.

Her dark brown hair fell around her shoulders in a mass of curls, framing an open, sweet face and lips that promised more than just smiles for the guy lucky enough to get to kiss them.

Brock suddenly felt like an awkward teenager. It took all his effort to arrange his face into a cool, confident smile. "Hello, ma'am," he said, putting on a slightly thicker drawl than usual. "I'm Brock McNeal. My folks live just over the way. They said Mrs. Stanford was in need of some help fixin' up this place, and I thought it best to come introduce myself."

A plan was already formulating in Brock's mind. Make nice to the old lady, get in good with the beautiful mystery woman, then ask her for a date. Easy enough.

The woman smiled. "Nice to meet you. Call me Cassie. Your mother was so sweet to offer your help."

Brock's mind shifted gears quickly. The widow was Cassie.

Before he could say anything, two young boys shot into the doorway, their identical faces peering at him from behind Cassie's legs.

"Zach, Carter, say hello to Mr. McNeal. He'll be helping us fix up the place a bit."

Brock tried his hardest to keep the disappointment off his face, but he wasn't sure he succeeded.

Of course she had kids. There had to be something or his mother would've just come out and told him about her sneaky little plan. She knew well enough by now he didn't plan on having any children, and that meant no dating women with kids, either.

Don't miss THE BULL RIDER'S TWIN TROUBLE
by Ali Olson, available January 2018
wherever Harlequin® Western Romance books
and ebooks are sold.

www.Harlequin.com

HWREXP1217

THE WORLD IS BETTER WITH

Romance

Harlequin has everything from contemporary, passionate and heartwarming to suspenseful and inspirational stories.

Whatever your mood, we have a romance just for you!

Connect with us to find your next great read, special offers and more.

f /HarlequinBooks

🐦 @HarlequinBooks

www.HarlequinBlog.com

www.Harlequin.com/Newsletters

Ⓗ HARLEQUIN®

A *Romance* FOR EVERY MOOD™

www.Harlequin.com